The Brume

J PATRICK LEMARR

WRITE CROWD PUBLISHING

For the burdened...
Matthew 11:28

"It may be that when we no longer know what to do, we have come to our real work."

WENDELL BERRY

Contents

As a speculative fiction author, I've had the opportunity to serve on panels with talented creatives like J. Patrick Lemarr. During the 2021 Imaginarium Convention in Kentucky, which is designed for such creatives, I stopped at Jeff's table and picked up his short story collection *All That Waits in the Night,* and won a copy of *Shadow Plays,* both of which introduced me to the character Dylan Drake.

Not only did I glimpse Jeff's marketing mind during that first conversation, but I also had the chance to meet his daughter who was manning the table alongside him. Over the next few years, I would happily learn of a minister's son's commitment to family, community, faith, and story. This man is a workhorse who knows how to world-build and create memorable moments within his world with clean, compelling, horror and fantasy stories. The strategies he comes up with for sharing those worlds and stories impresses me to no end.

Jeff's upbringing with Christian principles shines gently in his works, and *The Brume* is no exception. In it, he offers hints of hope and clarity where characters could otherwise give in to despair. Without being didactic, Jeff is able to present the idea that we have an all-loving Father who is the Author of all our stories; an Author who doesn't give up when the stakes rise in the second act. Through the wise Dylan Drake, Jeff offers a fallible yet heroic servant who travels to moments when he's needed most; a hero who steps out of the mist and dispels confusion.

Jeff's use of Dylan as a messenger throughout his stories is augmented in *The Brume* to warrior and I'm here for it. Jeff has offered a powerful view of the servant. For readers who have followed Dylan's adventures and assignments so far, Jeff's portrayal of the lad in this alternate Civil War history will surprise and energize you.

The Brume reflects Jeff's ability to wrap a recurring speculative-fiction character with supernatural heroism. Perfect for a world riddled with uncertainty and unrest, *The Brume* reminds us that the evil feeding off wars will be defeated in the end by the Author of all our stories. We can't lose hope. I welcome you, reader, to find entertainment and encouragement herein.

It was a privilege to read and enjoy an early version of *The Brume.* It was an honor to be asked to write a foreword introducing this installment in Dylan's journey through time and task…

Fantasy Author Sandy Lender
Proprietor, SandyLenderInk.com

THE EVERMORE

Beyond the boundaries of the world we know, there is a realm of impossible beauty, crafted from the dreams and imagination that fuels our mortal minds: the Evermore. At the heart of this realm lies the Great Library, a vast and expanding labyrinth of knowledge and wonder, which holds every story ever written within its walls. The agents of the Great Library labor to shape and guide the narratives of the world, editing history, and forging a brighter future. They act as both warriors and messengers, wielding sword and grace on behalf of the Author, all in the service of the greater story.

The Brume

Beaumont House, a sturdy blend of Greek Revival ambition and Southern farmhouse sense, stood beneath the live oaks and Spanish moss, still proud despite the years. Her buttercream paint was peeling, her porch rail broken by a spooked horse, but even war hadn't managed to steal her charm. Crooked shutters aside, she remained the envy of every family west of the Ocmulgee River.

Whether the specter creeping across the front lawn toward Beaumont House was a thick blanket of fog or the acrid smoke of a distant battlefield, young Olivia Beaumont could not determine. The ink-smudged sky suggested one; the faint thunder of cannon fire implied the other. Neither was within her power to change. Slender and fair, with honey-brown hair and soft blue eyes far older than her sixteen years, she closed the window and drew the curtains tight. Then she lit the lamps one by one, refusing to let the coming darkness swallow the home she loved.

Elizabeth Beaumont, two years her senior, ignored her sister's preparations and instead took quick stock of the pantry and cellar. The previous day's events had cast sudden doubt on whether they had provisions enough to last the fast-approaching winter. If they were besieged before the first snowfall, they might be left with little more than their meager stores.

George Beaumont III, eldest of the Beaumont siblings, was already securing the livestock and horses in case the weather—or war—turned even more foul. Tall and broad-shouldered despite his youth, he moved with the uneven gait forced on him by his ruined left leg. Each step dragged a little, though he disguised the worst of it with practiced dignity. The lamplight from the barn caught the sharp lines of his face—too tired for twenty-three—and the perpetual crease in his brow that responsibility had carved there. Cursing his useless knee, he worked as quickly as he could while keeping a wary eye on the fence line. If anyone brought the conflict to their door, it would fall to him to protect his sisters. Though he'd never admit such a thing to Elizabeth or Olivia, he felt ill-suited for the role of protector and lord of the manor, and had felt so long before a Derringer ruined his knee.

When his work was finished, he braced against his cane and made the long, aching walk back to the house. The world had fallen unnaturally still. Cannon fire—if that's what it had been—had ceased entirely. Fog curled thick around him, turning Beaumont House into a ghost beyond reach.

Then something stirred within the whiteness. A mass shifting its weight, patient and confident.

Unearthly.

A chill climbed George's spine. Nothing born of these woods moved like that.

"George Beaumont," someone said.

He turned and struck at the voice with his cane, but the young man who stood there caught it easily, his keen eyes fixed on the miasma ahead.

"I'm a friend," the stranger said. His clothes were ordinary—too plain for a man of station, yet not shabby enough for a beggar or thief. "And you are in terrible danger. There's something moving out there that means you harm."

George considered refusing—he'd been raised better than to trust a stranger at his doorstep—but the brume had carried a warning with it, a heaviness that still clung to his skin. And the boy before him had something unshakably calm in him, something that made George's fear ease by a hair.

"I'm unarmed," the stranger added, raising both hands, "and mean you no harm. But you *must* come with me, George. For your own safety."

George scanned the gloom once more.

Whatever shape he'd glimpsed had vanished, yet he felt it still—something primal, lurking just beyond sight, seeking whom it may devour.

"Where?" he managed.

"Back to the barn," the young man replied.

"We'll find no safety there," George whispered. "A strong breath would see the damned thing tumble."

"Trust me," the stranger said.

And, for reasons George could not name, he did. As he limped back toward the barn, the young man walked beside him, facing the fog, steps sure and steady as he moved backward.

When they reached the barn doors, something roared within the haze—a terrible, guttural bellow not born of any earthly throat. The sound rumbled so deep that George felt it in his sternum. He froze, certain death had come for him, his mind filled with thoughts of his beloved sisters.

At the sound of the roar, Olivia screamed—not just from fear, but from the sudden invasion of her mind. Images slammed into her all at once: blood-soaked earth, twisted limbs, mouths opened in silent terror. She felt an alien hunger—cold, deliberate, reveling in suffering—press against her thoughts, something that did not belong to her. In the marrow of her bones, she knew the violence in those images wasn't mere animal instinct. It was intentional.

Elizabeth rushed into the parlor with their father's Henry Repeating Rifle, but before she could ask why her sister had cried out, George crashed into the room, his cane skittering across the floor as he tumbled out of the closet. A stranger, younger than George's twenty-three years, landed beside him and slammed the door shut behind them.

Acting purely on instinct, Elizabeth leveled the rifle at the young man and pulled the trigger.

Nothing happened.

"Put that thing away, Lizzie," George said, fighting for breath. "He's a friend."

"He isn't," she snapped. "I know all your friends, George."

"He saved my life. He's earned the title."

"What happened, George?" Olivia asked, trying to help him stand. The stranger helped as well, retrieving George's cane from beneath the harpsichord and handing it over.

"I'm not sure, Ollie. Something was out there. Something monstrous. Could've been the devil himself for all I could see through the soup."

"I doubt it was the *actual* devil," the stranger offered, scratching the back of his head. "He tends to let other people do his dirty work."

Elizabeth narrowed her eyes. "Why were you in the linens?"

"I wasn't," George said. "We were in the barn. At least, we *were* before this fellow shoved me through the door."

"Sorry about the shove," the stranger said

awkwardly. "We were about to be eaten. A shove seemed less likely to ruin your day."

"Who are you?" Elizabeth demanded, lowering the gun.

"My name is Dylan, ma'am. Dylan Drake."

He stood straight as he said it—thin but not fragile, dark hair falling across a brow knit in concern. There was a steadiness to him, a quiet resolve that didn't match the youthfulness of his features.

His eyes, though, gave him away—bright, searching, and old in a way no boy's should be, as if he were never entirely where his body stood.

"And why are you here, Mr. Drake?"

"I'd like to know that answer as well," George said. "Not that I'm ungrateful."

"I came here hunting a desperate and dangerous creature," Dylan replied. "I hoped to stop it before it did any real damage, but…well, it's a lot bigger than I expected."

"What sort of creature?" Olivia asked.

"That's tough to answer, miss. It can sort of

become whatever it needs to be to get the job done."

"You speak in riddles," Elizabeth said. "Why should we trust this man, George?"

"As I said, Lizzie," George replied, sinking onto the harpsichord bench, "he saved my life."

"You only have *his* word for that."

"No, Lizzie. I know it—surely as I've ever known anything. Whatever is lurking out there in the mist is a danger to us all."

"I felt it coming," Olivia whispered. No one seemed to hear her but Dylan, who gave her a small, knowing nod.

"Where did you come from?" George asked.

"Let's just say I'm not from around here, George."

"That isn't good enough," Elizabeth insisted.

"Lizzie, let it go," Olivia said. "George trusts him. And so do I. I think the good Lord sent him our way."

"You are as simple as you are naïve, Ollie."

"Lizzie," George warned.

"Fine. Trust him if you feel inclined. I don't. I disagreed with the decision made yesterday and I disagree now. Mother and Father would certainly question us opening Beaumont House to strangers in a time of war. We barely have food enough for ourselves, George."

"I promise," Dylan said, "I'm not here for your food. I'm here to help you survive what's coming. You're all in great danger, Miss Beaumont. And that includes the two men you found yesterday."

At the mention of the two wounded men upstairs, George studied the young stranger's face.

"Who are you? How did you know we were sheltering those men? Are you a spy? A soldier?"

"I'm a helper, George. Nothing more."

"That isn't true," Olivia said, her eyes fixed on him. "You came out of the linen closet with George, but…George was out in the barn."

"I was," George confirmed. "We were. How did we get in the house?"

"Magic. Science. Miracle. Which are you least likely to doubt?"

"He's mocking us, George!" Elizabeth insisted.

"He isn't," Olivia countered. "Mr. Drake simply assumes we won't believe the truth."

Dylan smiled. "Very perceptive, Olivia."

"Please, call me Ollie."

Her hair was braided neatly into a bun, her plaid dress—her mother's last gift—falling in crisp pleats.

"Then feel free to call me Dylan," he said. "That goes for all of you."

George pressed. "Enough with the pleasantries. I'd like an actual answer to my question."

Dylan exhaled, rubbing the back of his neck.

"Fair enough. Just understand that the truth isn't going to sit comfortably. And knowing it may complicate things. But you've earned the right to hear it, especially considering what's happening in the world around you."

"You mean the war," George said.

"I do. The country is splitting itself apart,

and you and your sisters are caught in the middle."

"It's madness," Elizabeth said. "We don't want the Yankees stepping on state rights. They already reap the benefits of our resources without giving us an equal say in federal matters."

"But we also abhor slavery," Ollie added. The righteous anger burning behind her eyes sparked the same in her siblings. "We cannot fight—or stand—for a cause so rooted in the mistreatment of others. Both sides are corrupted."

"So you stayed out of the fight," Dylan said. "George's injury made that easier, but you took it further. Your parents taught you that kindness and grace were virtues of the highest order. You chose not to close your eyes to suffering, and you'd help neighbor or stranger in equal measure."

"That was George and Ollie," Elizabeth said. "Kindness doesn't require vulnerability. We can serve God without opening our home to—"

"Lizzie," George said gently. "Let him speak."

"This war between the states happened where I come from, too," Dylan continued. "It raged for nearly four years and changed our nation forever. But here, where *you* live, the war is in its ninth year because General Lee defeated Meade at Gettysburg. That victory led the Confederacy to form alliances with France and Belgium, and an influx of weapons that prolonged the conflict. What should have ended the war instead pushed it into a far bloodier chapter. For five more years, men have died. Ground won and lost. Cities burned."

"We aren't so removed from the world that we don't know what happens beyond our borders, stranger," Elizabeth grumbled.

"My point, Elizabeth, is that you and your siblings are living in a divergent stretch of history. The story of this world—of *this* United States—took a different turn than it did in mine."

"In *your* story?" Ollie repeated.

"Every life is a story," Dylan said. "Many of

them connected—some loosely, some tightly—forming an overarching narrative. One grand story that encompasses them all. It is the will of the Author."

"The Lord," Ollie murmured.

"He's called many things," Dylan said gently. "But yes. That name fits."

He glanced toward the fogged window as if listening for something beyond it.

"When He tells a story, He gives it room to breathe…room for us to *choose*. And sometimes people choose badly. They lose their way. So when a place grows too dark, He sends me in to remind folks that light still exists. That grace hasn't run out."

Elizabeth's fingers worried the edge of her sleeve.

"God does not send angels disguised as boys to frighten families in the night. If you claim otherwise, you mistake us for fools."

"No, ma'am. Not an angel. I'm just a man like any other. But I *have* been sent to help."

"Wait. Go back a bit," George said, brow

furrowing. "Are you saying this war was *meant* to end?"

"No. I'm saying in *my* story, it did. But this is an alternate tale. Things happened differently here, though I don't know why."

"You don't believe him, George. You can't possibly!"

"I do," Olivia said softly.

"You're a child," Elizabeth argued. "George?"

George raised a weary hand to still her. "You still haven't answered my original question, Dylan. How did we get back into the house?"

"Right...sorry. Got lost in the setup," Dylan said. "Every story that exists, George, exists in a place we call The Great Library. That's where I read about the creature out there and what was about to happen here. It's how I knew you'd need help."

He gestured toward the linen closet.

"From the Library, I can enter any story ever written. Any door can be a door that takes me where I need to go—well, not *any* door there, but I won't overcomplicate it. I opened the barn door there, and we stepped out of the linen closet here. We'd never have made it back on foot."

"That's impossible!" Elizabeth snapped. "You're a madman!"

"I can show you," Dylan offered, "but people like you tend not to believe what's beyond them…even after they see it firsthand."

"People like me?"

"Doubters," Ollie said flatly. "Complainers."

"Self-righteous know-it-alls," George added. He gave Dylan a nod. "But my sister is no simpleton. She's a stout-hearted girl. Show her. Give her a chance."

"I'm willing if she is."

Elizabeth handed her father's rifle to George and crossed her arms.

"Where to? The linen closet?"

"Fair enough place to start," Dylan said. "Where's a safe location we can exit from?"

"The cellar," George answered.

Dylan smiled and held out his hand. Elizabeth glanced at her brother and sister, searching their faces, then reluctantly placed her hand in his.

"If he absconds with me," she warned, "you'll both be to blame."

"If he were to kidnap you, Lizzie, you'd be promptly returned," Ollie said with a smirk. "No one can withstand your prattling for long."

Elizabeth ignored her and followed Dylan to the linen door. When he opened it, the shelves and folded linens were gone—replaced by a void, a depthless nothing that might lead anywhere.

She stood stiffly beside him, her hand clasped in Dylan's with a grip firmer than she intended. Loose strands of auburn hair had slipped from their pins and clung to her flushed cheeks, betraying the tension she tried to hide. Her hazel-green eyes flicked between the young stranger and the impossible void inside the linen closet, their usual sharpness softened by a fear she refused to name. A faint tremor ran through her arm where their hands met—proof that, for all her suspicion, she was too loyal to her brother and sister to step back now.

Before she could ask what had become of her mother's fine linens, Dylan pulled her gently forward. The darkness she expected lasted only a heartbeat. An instant later, she stepped out of the cellar door behind her siblings.

Ollie ran toward her, George hobbling behind on his cane.

"What happened?" Elizabeth asked.

"You went into the linen closet," Ollie replied, "and then popped out here."

"Same as what happened with me in the barn," George added. "Strange, isn't it?"

"Impossible," Elizabeth breathed as much as said.

"Clearly not, Lizzie. It just happened."

"But—"

"George is right," Ollie said. "Dylan proved himself. *Now* will you listen?"

Elizabeth nodded, still dazed.

"What's out there, Dylan?" Ollie asked. "I

felt it long before the fog rolled in. Something evil inching closer."

"I couldn't tell you exactly *what* it is, Ollie. Only that it feeds on death and misery. It came through a rip in the fabric of a world I was already working in."

George straightened. "Not this one?"

"No." Dylan shook his head. "I've been tracking the creature from story to story, hoping to cut it off before it found a place to root itself. The world it slipped through last…well, it bore some similarities to yours. Enough that I recognized certain patterns, certain dangers." He exhaled. "But not enough to know everything."

"It doesn't belong here," Ollie said quietly. "It's a danger to every story it passes through, isn't it, Dylan?"

"Exactly. Some worlds echo each other, even when their details diverge." He looked toward the fogged window. "Whatever damaged the veil between stories did so violently. The tear has spread chaos and death across several realities."

He turned back to them, his expression sobering.

"I've been sent here to help you three—and your two guests upstairs—survive the night."

Captain Gerald Meeks was not the best fighter pilot the navy had. Not by a long shot. He had tested near the bottom of his class at Naval Aviation Schools Command, but none of that meant he couldn't hold his own with the Pensacola boys as he cantered his A-4 Skyhawk into formation. He was capable, competent, and full of guts—just the way the brass liked them.

After a deadstick landing that could easily have ended his life in a JP-8 fireball, his fellow Bird Boys took to calling him Witch Doctor, a nickname he wore with pride. His official call sign was still "Chocks," thanks to an unfortunate training mishap, but off duty most of the boys preferred Witch Doctor.

On the day of his injury, he'd been flying a

training exercise over a civilian vessel bobbing off the Newport coast. Chatter suggested it was just a boondoggle for a visiting senator, but Meeks didn't mind. He loved his bird, and he loved the sky—at least until it opened like a gaping maw and swallowed him, plane and all.

Even if he had spotted the anomaly in time, he couldn't have avoided it, nor the unnatural energy radiating from it. The rift was too narrow for the Skyhawk to pass through intact. Its shimmering edge sliced into his starboard wing and aileron, sending the aircraft into an uncontrolled spin.

Comms were dead. The stick was dead. And if he didn't act within seconds, Cpt. Gerald Meeks would be dead. Unfamiliar terrain rushed up to meet him. He blew the canopy and ejected at the last possible heartbeat, unaware that the crippled Skyhawk was still banked hard, its one good wing reaching toward the sun. The chute deployed, but with his horizontal momentum, it barely slowed him.

There were sounds—the snapping of branches, the distant crash of his bird meeting earth. He felt cool air through the Nomex suit followed by the heat of exploding fuel some-where out of sight.

Then everything went black.

He woke to a world turned upside down. His head felt three sizes too big, and it took him a moment to realize it wasn't the world out of kilter, but him. He hung suspended from a tree by the chute's lines, trying to gather his bearings. Pain stabbed through his left shoulder; his right knee felt held together by rubber bands.

Where was the Coast Guard? For that matter, where was the coast? He'd been flying off Newport, but the terrain below was all wrong. No salt in the air—but something else. Something familiar.

Gunpowder.

"Help!" he managed. The effort nearly made him black out again. "Please…" This time the word barely rose above a whisper. "Please help me."

Somewhere in the distance, a dog howled.

He lost consciousness before he could call out again.

Per Dylan, the first order of business was securing every point of entry into Beaumont House. The danger wouldn't vanish with the dawn, but lasting through the night would at least give them a fighting chance of seeing what approached.

"Dylan and I can secure the windows upstairs," Ollie offered.

"Is this...*monster* able to climb?" Elizabeth asked, her new concern overpowering the shock she still felt from door-hopping with Dylan.

"The monster can become anything," Ollie said. "Dylan told us as much. So yes, if it wanted to. And not to brag, dear sister, but I've climbed in and out of my bedroom window more times than I can count."

"Ollie's right," Dylan said grimly. "Any opening that could let a person or animal through needs to be locked down nice and tight."

"Let me get you a hammer and a box of nails," George said. "If you can't secure the window, bar the door beyond it. Ollie, don't let him be precious about it. There's nothing he can scar that we can't repair."

Dylan smiled, nodded, and followed George to fetch the tools.

As soon as they were out of earshot, Elizabeth crossed her arms.

"You and George are far too trusting of this…Dylan."

"You saw what he did, Lizzie. You went with him between the linen closet and the cellar."

"It must have been a trick. An illusion. I saw similar things when the carnival passed through."

"If you need to believe that, Lizzie, then believe it. But you know what's happening here isn't of this earth. If we're to survive—"

"I'll do what needs doing," Elizabeth cut in. "But I have my limits."

"Just be kind to Dylan," Ollie implored her. "I sense…a weariness. If what he says is true—and I believe it is—he likely spends more time helping others than tending to his own life. That seems a terribly lonely way to live."

Elizabeth's expression warmed only a fraction before she smirked.

"Speak the truth, little sister. It's his handsome face you're drawn to, not his ridiculous story."

Ollie's cheeks reddened.

"It can be both at once," she said, unable to contain her smile.

"Ollie," George shouted from the dining room, "what became of my tools?"

"They're in the hall closet, George. Where I put them every time you leave them cluttering up the kitchen or the parlor or the dining room."

"Thanks, Ollie girl!"

Elizabeth's expression dimmed. "He leaves his cane beside his chair some mornings," she said quietly. "He forgets he needs it."

"Give him time," Ollie replied. "He's had so

much to manage since…well, since we've been on our own. He's too busy being strong for us and looking after the house to face the truth of his leg."

"This old house is falling to ruin, Ollie, but it's our home…and all we have left of mother and father. He needs to let us take on more of work."

She paused for a moment, willing away the tears threatening to emerge.

"He needs time to heal, Ollie. Caring for us and Beaumont House is *not* more important than his recovery. We need to convince George we can manage on our own. There are surgeons in the North who might help him."

Ollie shook her head. "While the war rages, the North is out of reach. Let's focus on surviving today and let tomorrow care for itself."

Dylan and George returned, each with a hammer in one hand and a bag of nails in the other.

"Ollie," George said, "once everything's secure upstairs, check on our guests. If their bandages need changing—"

"I can handle it," she assured him.

"—Lizzie or I can help you," he finished. "I don't want you in there alone for more than a quick look."

Ollie sighed and nodded.

<hr>

All the warrior remembered was the mist hovering like a spirit over the plains. The rest of his party, determined to destroy the creature that had ravaged their village, vanished into the formless white as if they had never existed. A chill threatened his spine, but he ignored it, narrowing his eyes at a strange movement to his left.

Before he could raise his knife, the paw of something impossibly fast struck his chest, hurling him to the earth with brutal force.

Stunned, he looked down at the wound: four deep claw marks carved nearly to the bone. Biting his lower lip, he pushed himself upright despite the pain. The beast had drawn first blood. Its predatory instincts would take hold now. It had wounded its prey. It would not retreat until it claimed its prize.

A sound like thunder rolled nearby just as his strength failed. He collapsed into the tall grass as a man shouted in a language he did not understand. A storm raged around him, but he whispered his thanks to the Lone Man—for his life, for his family, and for the years he had lived above the grapevine beneath the open sky.

As Dylan nailed the last upstairs window shut, he considered the night ahead. Survival would require every player working together. Ollie hadn't left his side. Curiosity moved her, yes—but there was something more.

"That's the last of them," he said, handing her the hammer. "Nothing's getting in up here."

"This creature you came to save us from," she said, "you said it isn't from this world?"

"Correct."

"And neither are you?"

"Also correct."

"But you seem so…" She hesitated.

He lifted an eyebrow.

"…*normal*, I suppose."

"My world is nearly the same as yours," Dylan said. "We declared independence from England. Relied on slave labor—much to our lasting shame. Even fought the war you're living through now. But it ended. We became, if not united, at least less eager to retread this awful ground. The world changed. So did we. Sometimes for good, sometimes for ill."

She stared at him, stunned. "You're from the *future*?"

"Of a very similar world to yours, yes." He paused. "Now, may I ask you a question?"

Her eyes narrowed, studying him. "Be my guest."

"How long have you had your gift?"

She stiffened. "What gift would that be, Dylan?"

"Don't kid a kidder, Ollie. Neither one of us is what anyone in either of our worlds would call normal. I bounce from story to story trying to bring a bit of hope to hopeless places, and you…what? Intuit? See things? How does it work?"

She smiled warmly and shook her head, sliding the toe of her shoe over the stained oak floor. Instead of meeting his eyes, she stared at the painting of her grandmother on the wall beside him.

"My siblings—God bless them—warned me to keep my curse a secret. Even from my parents."

"So George and Elizabeth *do* know," Dylan said gently, "even if they don't fully understand it."

"They wouldn't dare speak of it. Saying it out loud would make it too real. They love me, Dylan, but they've got enough to face already. My curse—"

"Why is it a curse?"

"What makes you call it a gift?"

She searched his face, hoping whatever he said next might quiet the anxiety she'd carried since the day her strange ability first appeared. There was a kindness in him that met her fear instead of magnifying it, and for a moment she almost believed it might vanish if she looked deep enough. When he spoke, it was with a certainty she could barely fathom.

"This ability of yours, Ollie, isn't a mistake. Not an accident of fate. The Author of your story wrote it into you for a *purpose.*"

"Which is?"

"That's not for me to explain," Dylan said with a wink. "Trust Him. When you need to know, you'll know. I promise."

Ollie blushed and looked away.

"Dylan, is there someone you…um, are you *courting* anyone?"

"Courting?"

Her face warmed. She didn't dare meet his eyes.

"Is courting not something you do in your world?"

He chuckled softly and stepped closer.

"It is," he said gently. "But, Ollie, I…don't really have time for it. Getting close enough to people to even consider such things isn't usually part of this job."

She nodded, suddenly feeling exposed.

"You're a lovely girl, Ollie. Smart, brave, gifted in extraordinary ways. But don't chase romance too soon. You might attach yourself to someone unworthy of you. Love will find you when it's time."

"This work you do…aren't you ever lonely?"

He smiled at her—warmly, sadly. Her insight impressed him. Her compassion even more.

"Sometimes," he admitted. "But the work I do doesn't allow for much free time."

"Surely you must rest."

"Of course. But when I'm not working, I go home, spend time with my mother. Go to school. Do all the normal-people things."

"Then you understand why I don't talk about my gift. Like you, I like to imagine I'm normal."

He nodded.

She hesitated, fingers curling lightly in her skirt, then drew a slow breath—gathering words she'd clearly never spoken aloud.

"My knowing doesn't come the same way

each time. Sometimes it's barely a tug—an intuition that won't leave me be. Other times it's a flutter of images, a brief glimpse of someone's heart…their past…or what waits for them down the road."

Her voice thinned.

"But when danger is near…like violence or…bitter, bone-deep hatred…it comes like a blow. A vision so sharp it knocks the breath out of me. Sometimes knocks me clear off my feet."

Dylan's expression softened with something like awe.

"And you've carried that alone? Ollie… with a war outside your window, and all the fear and grief that comes with it—you must *drown* in what you feel."

She shook her head, surprised at her own steadiness.

"If it *is* a gift," she said quietly, "*and* a burden… then the good Lord made me to bear it. Same as He's made you strong enough to carry what rests on *your* shoulders."

The words settled between them—gentle, honest, resolute.

Dylan studied her face a moment longer, and the mystery in his eyes deepened, not darkened.

"Normal could never do you justice, Ollie. You're extraordinary. And I'm honored to know you…even amid this madness."

As he said it, he brushed a bit of sawdust from her sleeve—nothing more than a practical gesture, yet his touch was so unexpectedly gentle that heat rushed to her cheeks.

For an instant, the room tilted. A flicker of sight—not quite a vision, not quite a dream—flared behind her eyes. A woman she'd never met: red hair caught in winter sun, a bottlecap button glinting like a tiny promise. Dylan stood beside her in that glimpse, older perhaps, steadier, his face bright with a kind of happiness Ollie had not seen on him.

The image vanished before she could breathe.

She swallowed, forcing herself to meet his gaze again.

"Normal or not," she said quietly, "*someone's*

going to see you, Dylan Drake. Truly see you. When it's time."

He blinked, puzzled—but she shook her head, letting the moment pass as though she'd said nothing unusual.

Dylan hesitated only a heartbeat, sensing the shift, then chose not to press her.

"Tell me about your wounded guests," he said gently.

"I don't know much," she replied, angling herself just enough that he wouldn't notice her blush. "The soldier wore a strange uniform. Not Yankee or Confederate. Before he woke, George guessed he might be a French spy, but he's certainly not French…and doesn't have the guile of a spy."

"And the native?"

"Just that—a native. Put quite the scare into Lizzie when he tried to get out of bed. Though my sister would be just as scared of a potato bug. He doesn't speak a word of English, so he's likely just as frightened of us as she is of him. George has dealt with several tribes when he traveled with Father, but this man doesn't speak any dialect George recognizes."

"That's fine," Dylan said. "My boss usually has a plan for those sorts of issues."

"You speak of God with a… familiarity that's foreign to me."

"I didn't mean to offend. And I promise it isn't disrespect. On the contrary, knowing the Author as I do…seeing the lengths He'll go to bring hope to the hopeless, to extend grace to even the most difficult of—"

Her face twisted into such bafflement he couldn't help but laugh.

"I'm sorry," he said. "My point is this: like you, I haven't seen Him face-to-face. That time will come soon enough for all of us. But I've learned to trust Him. I've come to think of Him as a trusted confidant… and a friend. My lack of formality is—"

"The stuff of family. I understand," she replied, a faint smile settling on her lips.

As George finished nailing the kitchen door closed, Elizabeth stood at the parlor window. She saw nothing but the swirling white vapor blanketing the landscape. Though she'd never confess it to her siblings, she too felt the unseen danger pressing against the walls of Beaumont House.

The last few years had been merciless—first their parents' deaths, then George being wounded while defending her from the consequences of her own misjudgment. Elizabeth carried the blame quietly, the way she carried most things.

George had always been the stalwart one: dutiful son, protective brother, respected citizen. Without their parents, she and Olivia had leaned on him for safety, for routine, for the illusion that life might one day return to something whole. Elizabeth feared that one foolish romance had cracked that fragile balance beyond repair.

"Penny for them, Lizzie," George said.

She startled. She hadn't realized he was

there, hammer and nails in hand. Embarrassed, she lied.

"I was wondering whether this creature you and your little urchin fortuneteller are so worried about is worth all the damage we're doing to Beaumont House."

"*We* are Beaumont House, Lizzie," George said gently. "You, me, and Ollie. This old place is just the box that keeps the storms outside. Or, in this case, the monsters."

"So you want us to abandon it? George, it's our inheritance."

"I didn't say abandon it," he replied. "But if it comes down to this house or you and Ollie, I'll let it burn."

She turned away so he wouldn't see the tear threatening to escape.

"Lizzie?"

"Do what you think is best, George," she said quietly. "Ollie and I trust you."

He pressed a kiss to the back of her head before limping toward the hall.

"I'm going to put the tools away before

Ollie gets cranky about them again. Can you go help her check on our other guests?"

She wiped her eyes with the back of her hand, drew in a steadying breath.

"Of course."

<hr>

Captain Gerald Meeks could still feel the shard of metal lodged in his left shoulder. His right knee throbbed—broken or dislocated, he couldn't tell. The room was dim save for the oil lamp beside his bed. Every instinct screamed that danger was close, but he was in no condition to face it.

The girl who'd found him had bandaged the wound and sterilized it with whiskey, but every shift of his arm sent pain lancing through him. That metal needed removal, and he doubted his hosts had the medical training for the job.

When the door creaked open, he tried to sit up but lacked the strength. Two teenage girls stepped inside carrying a pitcher of water and some rags.

"You're awake," the younger noted. "How are you feeling?"

"Like hell," he muttered.

"Please watch your language," the older said sharply.

He nodded, mumbling an apology.

"Were you able to reach my XO?" he asked. "Or anyone on the Truman?"

"The nearest telegraph is in Atlanta," the younger explained. "There's little hope of getting word to your regiment, soldier. Especially tonight."

"Telegraph? You don't understand," Meeks said. "My boat may not know I punched out. I've gotta RTB with due haste, little miss, or else my ass is grass."

"Sir," the older warned, "if you continue to be offensive, we'll leave you to tend your own wounds. I imagine you'd want that bandage changed."

"I'm sorry. Truly. I just…need to get in touch with my squad."

"We'll do all we can," the younger said,

peeling back the bandage. "Let us start with clean dressings and move on from there, yes?"

At the sight of the injury, both girls flinched.

"It's bad, isn't it?" Meeks said, refusing to look. "You gotta get me a real medic. I appreciate what you've done, but if we're dealing with infection—"

"Can I have a look?"

The voice came from the doorway. The man standing there wasn't dressed as finely as the girls, but that wasn't what caught Meeks's attention. There was something else—something he couldn't name, but he clocked it immediately.

Something that set Meeks's instincts humming.

"Are you a doctor now?" the older girl asked.

"No, Elizabeth," he replied, "but I happen to know a *great* physician. I've picked up a thing or two. If you ladies would give me the room, I'd like to see what I can do. Do you mind, Ollie?"

The younger girl shook her head and set the fresh bandages at the foot of the bed. Elizabeth placed the pitcher on the bureau, shot the young man a warning glare, and swept out after her sister.

Once they were gone, the young man stepped to the bedside and smiled at the wounded pilot.

"Captain Meeks, my name is Dylan Drake. And you're a long, *long* way from home."

"I had that feeling," Meeks muttered. "Last thing I remember, I was flying some fool's errand off Newport. Hit something invisible. Next thing I know, I'm waking up in Amish country."

Dylan chuckled. "Not Amish. And what you hit wasn't exactly invisible. It was a portal of sorts—a rip in the fabric of reality."

Meeks narrowed his eyes.

"Am I on some hidden camera show or something? Because I promise you, son, I am very wounded, and this shit is not funny."

"I know it sounds impossible, Captain. But it's the truth. Your flight took place in 1995. June, if I'm remembering correctly."

"July second," Meeks corrected automatically. "Why? What day is it now? How long was I out?"

"Today is May the seventeenth of 1869. The Civil War is still raging…though it should have ended years ago."

Meeks stared.

"Sure, kid. Pull the other one."

"I'm deadly serious. You crashed through a tear between worlds and landed in an alternate history." Dylan took a breath. "I can get you home, but we've got a few things to deal with first."

"Let's say I believe you." Meeks held up a hand. "I don't—but let's pretend I do. How does some Antebellum kid know all this?"

"*Antebellum* means 'before the war,' Captain," Dylan corrected gently. "But I'll answer your question. I'm from even further down the timeline than you are. The *original* timeline— where the war ended in April of 1865 and the nation could finally heal. The difference between us is that I came here willingly."

"And why's that?"

"To get you home," Dylan said, "and to help these good people survive what's waiting out there in the fog."

"Your story is tango uniform, full stop, kid," Meeks said. "But I'll be damned if I didn't feel something coming. I've been pinging a bogey since I woke up, and I knew it wasn't those two little girls. Whatever's out there has a real high pucker factor."

"We'll make it if we stick together," Dylan assured him. "But first, we've got to get you on your feet."

"Then I hope you've got a miracle in your back pocket, kid."

Dylan smiled faintly.

"You know what, Captain Meeks? I just might."

"What do you think he's doing in there?" Elizabeth asked, leaning against the wall outside the room where the stranger,

Dylan Drake, had asked to speak to their wounded guest alone.

"He wants to help him," Ollie said around a yawn. "Why are you so suspicious, Lizzie? He saved George and showed you what he can do. Maybe he can help that poor soldier in ways we can't."

"So you think he's what? Some sort of magician? A faith healer?"

"I don't rightly know what he is," Ollie admitted. "But he's powerful, Lizzie. More than he lets on. And he's good. And kind. And lonely. I can feel that, too."

"You always think the best of people."

"No, I don't. I treat everyone with kindness—that's not the same thing as assuming they're harmless. You know I have…an instinct. When I say he's good and we can trust him, I mean I *know* it. As sure as I know you love me even when you pick at me. Or that George is the strongest man I know, despite his leg." Her voice caught, just for a moment. She swallowed and went on. "He'd fight the world for us. He'd lay down his life."

"I worry for George," Elizabeth said quietly. "I challenge him because—"

"Because if you didn't, he'd think you were going easy on him."

Elizabeth nodded, the admission softening her expression.

"We're a mess, aren't we, Lizzie? I'm strange. George is wounded. And you're—"

"A cold fish."

Elizabeth met her sister's gaze, daring her to deny it. But Ollie's eyes held only love.

"You keep people at arm's length to protect yourself," Ollie said gently. "It feels safe. Caring brings pain. You're not wrong about *that*, Lizzie. But it also brings joy. And it's through other folks' hands and feet that the good Lord often moves."

"I'm tired of being afraid, Ollie. Tired of worrying."

"I know. And now we've got a new reason to be afraid stalking around out there in the dark. But Dylan is as good as his word. If you can't trust him yet, then trust *me*. We're safest with him on our side."

"I do, you know," Elizabeth replied. "Trust you, I mean. I may pick at you a lot, but—"

She never finished the thought. Ollie stepped forward and wrapped her arms around her, warm and sure, leaving no need for further explanation.

"You're saying there's a monster outside," Captain Meeks said, trying to absorb everything Dylan had told him. "One that can look human. Like the Terminator."

"It's not a machine," Dylan said. "But it's dangerous. And yes, it can take any form. Not just human."

Meeks shook his head. "I've flown into worse briefings than this—but they usually came with a diagram."

"Sorry. No diagrams tonight," Dylan said.

"It's a lot to swallow, kid. Portals, time travel, monsters in the midst of the mist."

"*Very* alliterative," Dylan noted.

Meeks snorted. "My pops was an English

prof. Taught Dickens and Brontë at a little community college. Every now and then I try to say something smart enough to make him look down and smile."

"I'm sure he is," Dylan said quietly.

A fresh wave of pain rolled through Meeks, forcing a wince. "Unless you've got that miracle you mentioned, I may be seeing him sooner than planned."

"Well, 'sooner' is a relative term," Dylan said. "But let's just say… not today. And hopefully what I'm about to do will buy me a little trust."

Meeks frowned. "What exactly are you going to do?"

Dylan smiled—bright, earnest, and unshakably calm.

"I'm gonna ask for an edit."

George could see nothing in the brume beyond the leaded glass of the kitchen door. No monsters. No soldiers in blue or gray looking to claim Beaumont House. And no help coming that wasn't already inside.

Still, something in his chest ached. Life as he knew it was changing. Ollie's condition was one thing. But the boy, Dylan, was something else entirely. Together, they hinted at a larger reality his education had not prepared him for. Other worlds. Other wars. Whatever came in the night, he would never see the world the same.

He was pulled from his thoughts when Elizabeth came downstairs, looking as though she'd swallowed a scream.

"What troubles you, Lizzie?"

"Nothing. Your mystery man is performing some sort of hocus-pocus on the soldier. I suppose he'll deal with the savage next."

"Lizzie," George said, quiet but firm, "if *any* man is a savage, *all* men are. And yet Scripture says we were made in the image of our Creator. Is He a savage in your eyes?"

Elizabeth folded her arms. "Of course not."

"Then see in our native guest the same

image of God you see in me—or in yourself. He deserves what grace we can offer."

"You and Ollie are saints, then. What does that make me?"

"Tired," George said warmly. "And worried. Your words run ahead of you when you are. Mother always knew."

Despite herself, Elizabeth smiled.

"What was it you'd borrowed without her permission, Lizzie? Her locket?"

"Her perfume." Her cheeks flushed.

"Ah, yes," he said, chuckling softly.

"I wanted to impress little William Bairnes, of all people. He used to wait for me outside the mercantile. I thought rose water might win his heart."

"Did it?"

She stuck her tongue out at him, which made him laugh.

"She punished you with my chores, if I remember."

"Two weeks," Elizabeth said, shaking her head. "It took me *days* to feel clean again."

"I didn't fare much better. Mother stuck

you with my chores, so I took yours. Peeled potatoes till my thumb went raw."

Elizabeth laughed harder at the thought of him fumbling through kitchen work while she tended the livestock. All over half an ounce of toilet water.

"I love you, George. And I'm glad you know me well enough to see my sharp tongue isn't who I truly am."

"Lizzie, no matter your mood, I know you to be kind of heart and mighty in spirit. My correction isn't judgment—only a reminder others don't know you as I do."

"It's why I need you and Ollie. To file down my rougher edges."

"We need *each other*," he said. "The whole of us is more than the sum of our dreams and talents. Beaumonts aren't built for solitude."

"I know, George."

"That doesn't mean I won't bless a man worthy of you. Martin Tolliver simply wasn't that man."

"Your poor leg proves that," Elizabeth whispered. "I...I'm so—"

"Don't you dare apologize. You didn't pull a Derringer in the middle of a scuffle. Tolliver alone bears that shame."

"George—"

"And I'm to blame for letting my fists do my talking. I'm usually more clear-headed."

"He besmirched my honor. You did what any good brother would."

"Father would have found another way," he admitted.

"Father wasn't there," she replied. "You were. And despite the affection I once had for Martin, I was never prouder to be your sister than in that moment. If I'd known he would shoot you—"

"You couldn't have known, sister mine."

"Thankfully he was as poor a shot as he was a man, or you might've died."

"Truthfully, Lizzie," George said with a grin, "I thank him. That lead ball has improved my dancing considerably."

She laughed, and he joined her—and the weight each carried felt, for a moment, a bit lighter.

Olivia Beaumont was pressing her ear to the door when it swung open, nearly startling her out of her shoes. She gasped and staggered back, only to feel a steadying hand on her elbow. Dylan laughed softly, keeping her from colliding with the plant stand behind her. The warmth of his touch sent color rushing to her cheeks.

"You startled me, Dylan!"

"I didn't mean to, Ollie. I was coming to tell you Captain Meeks is doing much better. I hoped to check on your other guest."

"Better? But his wound was—"

"Disgusting? Yes. Teetering on infection? Also, yes. But the Author of his story had other plans—for our situation and for the good Captain's future."

"You're a wonder, Dylan."

"I'm just a man, Ollie. Flesh and blood, prone to mistakes like everyone else."

"How old *are* you? Older, I suspect, than you look."

"I'll turn eighteen shortly," he said. "Traveling as much as I do lends me an air of maturity, I suppose. But don't let that fool you. I'm still just a kid. No different than you, really."

"My world is quite singular, Dylan. It always has been."

"But your place in it is no less important, Ollie."

She smiled at that. His kindness was genuine. It radiated from him without guile. He carried no hidden motives. Only grace, and a fierce determination to do good.

"What can you tell me about the other gentleman?" Dylan asked.

"It seems he was attacked by a bear or something," she said, leading him toward the next room. "He was pale and barely breathing when George found him. It's only by God's grace he's still among the living."

"I suspect you're right."

The vision struck Ollie without warning. Her knees buckled, and Dylan lunged to catch her before she hit the floor. Her body seized in his arms, eyes rolling back as images—unyielding, certain—flashed across her mind. Not possibilities. Truths.

When the vision released her, she slumped against him and began to weep.

"Ollie, what is it? What did you see?"

She shook her head violently. Speaking the truth would make it real, and she could not bear that—not yet.

"Slow breaths," Dylan murmured, one hand steadying her head. "You're going to hyperventilate. You're safe. I've got you."

She followed his instruction, breath by breath, until the trembling eased. When she looked up at him, her smile was faint but sincere.

She liked Dylan Drake—not for the reasons Lizzie teased her about, but for the ease with which he cared for others. She knew, bone-deep, that if it came down to saving himself or saving her, her siblings, or their wounded guests, he would choose sacrifice without hesitation. His courage did not come from believing himself invincible, but from trusting his Author to let nothing befall him without purpose—and to use even pain for good. That faith anchored him. She hated to think she would be the tempest to test it.

"I think I'll wait here," she whispered. "There's a chair by the window near the stairs. Would you bring it?"

"Of course," he said, helping her to her feet.

He fetched the chair and set it beside her. She sat carefully, still steadying her breath.

"I'm sorry," she said. "I never know when that's going to happen. It's earned me more bruises than I care to count."

"I'm just glad I was there to catch you," he replied. "I'm going to tend to the warrior's wounds now, but don't think for a moment we're done talking about what you saw."

"I know," she said just above a whisper. "But it can wait a little longer, I promise."

He nodded and stepped away, doing his best to hide the worry tightening behind his eyes.

The warrior had awakened once to the chaos of a pale, screaming female, then surrendered again to the darkness. Though consciousness eluded him, he felt gentle hands tending his wounds—cleaning them, binding them. A man's voice, strong yet concerned, told him all would soon be well.

And the Lone Man spoke.

He warned that the great beast who had struck him in the mist was still hunting and endangering the Nup'tadi both above and below the earth. But another would come, the Lone Man said. A hunter and protector who would lead the fight. And that man would need the warrior's help.

In his fevered dreams, he saw the creature's form shifting—seeking to hide among those it hunted. Fierce, yet afraid. Afraid of the protector.

Then a voice called to him in the tongue of his people, and in the dream he ran toward it. His soul longed for home. He prayed the Lone Man would let that voice guide him back to his tribe.

The voice persisted, drawing him upward from the dream, urging him to take courage and prepare for war. When at last he opened his eyes, the world swam into focus, and he found himself staring up at a pink-skinned young man speaking the language of his ancestors.

Pathmaker tried to sit and failed. Only then did he feel the weight of his body again: the broad sweep of his chest, now tightly bandaged; the heavy braids of his black hair slipping across his shoulders; the warmth of blood returning to limbs that should have been too wounded to move. His skin—deep umber and marked with the faint scars of earlier hunts—gleamed with sweat. Even weakened, he carried the unmistakable bearing of a warrior: powerful arms, a proud line to his jaw, and dark, steady eyes that took in the stranger with equal parts confusion and defiance.

"Don't be afraid," the stranger said gently. "You were hurt, but all is well now."

[You are not Nup'tadi,] the warrior replied, his voice rough with pain. [How is it you speak the language of my people?]

"I don't," the stranger answered. "But we've been given the gift of understanding one another. What is your name, my friend?"

[My name is Pathmaker. I was hunting with my brothers when a great beast came through the milky air and tore me open.]

"My name is Dylan. The creature that harmed you is still out there, and the family who cared for you is in grave danger. I will need your help, Pathmaker, to hunt the beast and to get you home."

Pathmaker nodded, running his fingers across the scars on his chest. There was no pain.

[There is healing in your hands, Dylan. The Lone Man must have sent you.]

Dylan smiled.

"I'll come back for you, Pathmaker. Rest and regain your strength. When the time comes to face all that waits in the night, I'll need you at your best."

[I will prepare myself, within and without. The Lone Man will walk with us.]

As Dylan stepped from the room, Ollie sat up straighter in her chair, trying—and failing—

to hide the sorrow tensing her features. She shaped it into a fragile smile as Dylan approached. He knelt before her, mindful of the era's proprieties but more mindful of her trembling hands, which he gently took in his own.

"Ollie," he said, searching her eyes. "Talk to me."

The warmth of his hands summoned tears to the corners of her eyes. His kindness steadied her, yet she knew the moment had to follow the path shown in her vision.

"How is Pathmaker?" she asked.

Dylan lifted an eyebrow, ready to ask how she knew his name—until her expression reminded him. Her gift. Of course.

"He's fine," he said. "Healed."

"How?"

"Same as Captain Meeks. The Author intervened."

"You had some part to play, surely."

"Only to trust," Dylan replied. "And ask Him to have His way in the moment."

"I trust Him, too," she whispered. "Which is why I don't want to tell you what I saw. But I know I must. For your sake. And for George and Lizzie." She swallowed hard. "They'll be so scared, Dylan."

Dylan stared into her blue eyes, shimmering with tears she refused to release. Something inside him weakened. Doubt, always lurking beneath the surface, pressed upward despite all the miracles he'd witnessed, all the battles he'd survived.

He didn't return the girl's crush, but he cared for her deeply. Seeing her suddenly afraid wounded him. He prayed silently for courage—not only to hear what she would say, but to face what must follow with his gaze fixed upon the Author's will.

"Tell me, Ollie," he whispered. "Whatever you saw, I won't falter in my duty."

"I know."

She kissed his forehead, then bent to his ear and whispered all she had foreseen—slow, steady, leaving nothing out. It took longer than he expected, long enough for the silence between her sentences to bruise him more deeply than the words themselves. By the end, the young man who had stood against nightmare after nightmare was openly weeping.

When her whisper faded, he looked up through wet, stunned eyes. And beneath the hurt, anger caught fire.

"Ollie," he managed, "I *won't* let that happen."

"Yes, you will."

"I came here to—"

"I know," she said, her own tears finally falling at the sight of his. "But my story is my own, Dylan. And your authority—impressive as it is—is *finite*. And rightly so. You can only see what you're allowed to see."

"There must be *something* I can change," he pleaded, swiping at his face with the back of his sleeve. His mind spun, hunting for any path that might subvert what she had described.

"Don't you dare," she said, gently taking his chin in her palm. "You are a fine human being, Dylan Drake. But like all of frail humanity, you'd make a terrible, tyrannical god. As would I. Let the good Lord finish my story. I trust

Him. So do you. Don't let grief make you forget it."

His breath hitched. His eyes darted, searching hers for some answer to the fear threatening to undo him.

"Dylan," she continued, "your calling hasn't changed. You're still meant to face what stalks the darkness. Still meant to obey the Author. In my vision, I saw you doing exactly that—sword in one hand and Captain Meek's pistol in the other, being who you are. And that gave me the strength to do what I must."

She touched her forehead to his. "Do not falter now, or you'll steal what little courage I have."

He swallowed the lump in his throat and nodded.

"What should I do?" he asked.

"Explain to Captain Meeks and Pathmaker what must be done," she said. "I'll go to George and Elizabeth and tell them we need to pack what matters and leave the rest behind."

He nodded, still praying for another way.

Ollie gave him a gentle, sorrowful smile and kissed his forehead once more.

"Stand up," she said gently. "You've got work to do. And remember what I've told you. You mustn't change *anything*. Even when it looks grim."

"Yes, ma'am," he replied, rising and sniffing hard before offering her his hand. "I'll do my part."

"I know," she said, taking it as she stood. "And I'll do mine. Thank you, Dylan."

He had no words left, only the ache in his chest and the prayer stirring within him. He watched as she descended the stairs, stepping back into what remained of her story.

***

Captain Gerald Meeks had seen plenty of strange things even before the Navy. What the boy, Dylan Drake, had done, however, was a new category of unbelievable. Though never much of a praying man, Meeks had always believed in a higher power—just not one that aligned neatly with his Roman Catholic upbringing.

But he'd seen it with his own eyes: the wound in his shoulder sealing shut as the boy whispered a prayer. The shard of metal—sharp and agonizing moments earlier—bubbled away and vanished as if it had never existed. His dislocated knee had snapped back into place, warming with whatever miracle was crawling through his bloodstream at Dylan's request.

Now, less than ten minutes later, he was standing rejuvenated and free of pain.

Captain Meeks cut a solid, steady figure—tall and broad-shouldered, his Navy flight suit scuffed from the crash and streaked with smoke. His close-cropped hair and square jaw spoke of discipline, but there was a looseness behind his eyes that suggested he wasn't above the occasional late night in the officers' lounge, swapping stories over something stronger than coffee. Even restored to full health, he carried himself with the wary readiness of a man who'd learned to expect trouble and meet it head-on.

A battle was coming, the boy had said. He needed to be ready.

It was a lot to process—portals, monsters, and a Civil War–era siege—but the kid had a way about him. Meeks believed him despite the absurdity. Whatever was coming, he intended to stand his ground.

As if sensing that very thought, Dylan returned. Something in him had shifted; he looked shaken, wounded in spirit though untouched in body.

"Things have taken a turn," Meeks said. "What's the sit-rep, kid?"

"You have a sidearm, Captain?"

"Always. Standard-issue emergency gear. Am I gonna need it?"

"I'm going to ask for it," Dylan said, extending his hand.

"No offense, kid," Meeks said, "but handing a loaded pistol to someone I barely know is usually how my ass ends up in a sling."

He studied Dylan more closely now.

"And judging by the look in your eye,

you're planning to do something heroic and terminal."

Dylan didn't answer right away.

"Not something stupid, though," he said at last. "Something necessary. I'll return it promptly. You'll need it soon enough."

Meeks searched the boy's face, found no guile there, and handed over the gun.

"You know how to work a Sig?"

"I've handled my share of guns," Dylan said. "I prefer a sword when I can choose—but this will do."

"I'm hardly a proficient shot. If you've got the knack, it's better in your hands."

"No," Dylan said gently. "This is only a loan."

"Whatever you say. How's the other guest?"

"Healed. Ready."

"How much time do we have?"

The answer came in the form of a thunderous crash from downstairs. Beaumont House shuddered. Pictures fell from the walls. Fine china shattered in the cabinet George Beaumont II had built with his own hands.

And then Elizabeth screamed—high, sharp, and blood-curdling—followed by two gunshots.

"None," Dylan replied.

***

Ollie had been explaining to Elizabeth and George why they needed to evacuate the home their grandparents built—why they had to follow Dylan and the native he called "Pathmaker" into the mist—when the southeast corner of Beaumont House tore open as easily as a child ripping through Christmas paper.

It happened so fast there was no time to scream. The beast surged through the opening, snatched young Olivia Beaumont, and vanished back into the swirling night before either sibling could move.

Elizabeth's scream shattered the stillness, sharp enough to wake the dead. George grabbed his father's Henry Repeating Rifle and fired two blind shots into the mist.

"George," Elizabeth gasped, gripping his arm, "did you see it?"

"Not clearly," he panted. "It wasn't shaped right. Too many limbs…or not enough."

He swallowed hard, still staring into the brume. "And the fog— it moved with the creature. Like it was a part of it."

Elizabeth shuddered. "There was a light inside it, too. Blue. Flickering. Like lightning trapped in water."

As she spoke, Dylan Drake came pounding down the stairs with the Captain's sidearm, followed by Meeks and the native warrior, Pathmaker.

"What the hell happened?" Meeks barked.

"It took Ollie," Elizabeth gasped, eyes locking onto Dylan. "That thing you warned us about—it took her. Where were you?"

"Doing what she asked of me," Dylan replied, staring past all of them toward the torn-open corner of the house and the darkness beyond. "We need to go."

"You mean to follow them," George said, rifle still raised. "If we move now—"

"George," Dylan said firmly, "Ollie made me promise to get you and Elizabeth to safety. That's what I intend to do."

"We can't just leave her!" Elizabeth cried.

"She saw all of this!" Dylan shouted back, his composure finally cracking. "The shock knocked her off her feet. She *knew* she'd be taken. She was terrified, Elizabeth—shaken to her bones. And her only thought was of you and George."

"What?" George lowered his rifle, stunned. "What are you saying?"

"She had a vision," Dylan said, trying to steady his breath. "She told me what was going to happen."

"And you didn't stop it?" George demanded.

"She told me I *couldn't*. She said I'd only make things worse if I interfered. Her story was always going to end here. She told me to let it happen and do my job."

"Your *job* was to protect us, you coward!" Elizabeth screamed. "To protect *her!*"

"You want to hate me, Elizabeth? Go ahead," Dylan shot back. "But Ollie made me promise to save you, and I'll do it—even if I have to drag you along kicking and screaming."

"Easy, kid," Meeks said, placing a steady hand on Dylan's shoulder. "They've had the hell scared out of them. And judging by that hole, I'd say their fear is justified."

"George," Dylan continued, forcing his voice calm, "Ollie foresaw that a siege wasn't a viable option. No matter what we tried, staying in Beaumont House was going to be the end of us. The *only* path to safety is to do what the creature won't expect—venture out into the night."

"To die?" George asked.

"No," Meeks answered for him. "To find a portal out of this joint. That's the plan, right?"

"That's right," Dylan confirmed. "Path-maker will lead the way."

Elizabeth shook her head violently. "I won't follow him, George. We can't leave Ollie."

Dylan's face hardened.

"Ollie is dead!" he spat. "She foresaw her end coming. There will be time to mourn her, but it's not now. If we stop here, the Beaumont line ends tonight."

"How dare you?" George growled, seizing Dylan by the collar. "Who do you think you are?"

[Remove your hand from the Lone Man's prophet,] Pathmaker warned, stepping forward.

"Relax," Dylan said quickly to the warrior, then to George, "Please. Let me explain."

George released him but kicked an overturned table aside in frustrated grief.

"This *wasn't* my plan," Dylan said, voice tight. "I thought we could hole up here—survive the night, regroup at dawn. But Ollie… saw something different. She said we wouldn't make it if we stayed."

"And you think she knew that… ungodly thing was coming for *her*?" George demanded.

"She told me so," Dylan answered through clenched teeth. "She also said that if you or Elizabeth doubted me, I should say the name *Thurston*. I don't know what it means, but—"

Elizabeth went still. "You aren't lying," she whispered. "She would never have given you that name unless she needed us to believe you."

"I don't get it," Captain Meeks said. "What's a 'Thurston'?"

"A boy," George said quietly, raking his trembling fingers though his hair. "He went to school with Olivia. He was the first person she ever had a vision about. She kept it a secret from our parents—said Mother and Father wouldn't understand."

"She knew *we* didn't really understand either," Elizabeth admitted, tears welling. "But she told us anyway. She…she needed our help. She'd always kept *our* secrets, so she trusted us with hers."

"What had she seen?" Dylan asked.

"Thurston being trampled by a startled horse," George said. "I thought she'd gone mad. She begged me to intervene. She knew the day and the hour it would happen. She was so desperate I finally agreed. I had never seen her in such a state."

"Did you save him?" Meeks asked.

"He tried," Elizabeth answered, having noticed her brother's voice beginning to break. "But when George got to town, he learned Thurston was sick—still in bed. Seemingly in no danger at all."

"I felt foolish," George admitted. "I left planning to go home and give Ollie a piece of my mind, but—"

"But it happened," Dylan said. "And I'm guessing it was exactly as she foresaw."

George nodded, jaw tight.

"Thurston had a crush on Ollie," Elizabeth added. "He overheard George speaking with his mother and snuck out the back door to catch him. We never did learn what spooked the horse."

George closed his eyes, shaking his head. "I think he just wanted me to give Ollie a message from him."

"I'm sorry, George," Dylan said. "For all of it."

Elizabeth continued, "Ollie never mentioned Thurston again. She didn't want us to feel guilty for not believing her. She only told you about him to make sure we listened this time." She wiped her eyes. "We didn't trust her then. We had better now."

George squared his shoulders. "Tell us what you need us to do. You won't have any more trouble from us."

Dylan nodded and turned to Pathmaker.

"The beast will return," he told the warrior. "I need you to lead us through the fog."

[I do not know this land,] Pathmaker replied. [Nor the path back to my people.]

"Trust the Lone Man to guide you."

The warrior's eyes hardened with purpose.

[You are the protector. I am the warrior. My destiny lies with the beast. You said the girl lifted the veil of what is to come. Did she tell you this?]

Dylan nodded.

"What's he saying?" Meeks asked.

"You spoke to him," George said. "And he understood you?"

"We understand *each other*, yes."

"And he's going to get us out of here?" Elizabeth asked.

Dylan's throat tightened. He hated the deception but keeping them alive meant following Olivia's final instructions without deviation.

"We follow his lead," he said, forcing the words out evenly. "It's our only chance."

As George and Elizabeth gathered the few heirlooms they could carry, Captain Meeks stood guard at the gaping wound in Beaumont House. Rifle shouldered, he scanned the mist for movement.

Pathmaker sat at the kitchen table, sharpening his axe on the wet stone George once used to put a keen edge on his mother's carving knife. The slow scrape of metal on stone grated at Dylan's frayed nerves. The warrior noticed, paused mid-stroke, and regarded him.

[Do you doubt the girl?]

Dylan looked up. His eyes carried grief and

anger, warring like two storms beneath the surface.

[Or is it the Lone Man you now doubt?]

"No offense, Pathmaker," Dylan said tightly, "but you don't *know* me. You have no idea what I carry. How many times my 'help' costs a life. How often I come to care for people I know I'll have to leave when the work is done."

[You feel sorry for yourself. Do you expect my pity?]

Dylan shot to his feet so quickly the chair toppled backward, clattering across the floor.

"Be careful," he warned. "I'm a patient man, but not right now."

Pathmaker's expression did not change.

[You claim to trust the girl. You told her people you do. Yet your anger reveals it to be a lie. If you truly trusted her, you would have no anger.]

"She was a kid," Dylan said, fighting to keep his voice level. "She may have been right, but that doesn't make any of this *fair*."

[What is fair under the sun, young one?

Fair is a mortal conceit—a comforting lie. There is only what is, and what is not. Ever has it been so. Your doubt, then, is directed higher. At the Lone Man, I think.]

Dylan lifted the fallen chair, setting it back on its legs. He sank into it slowly.

"Don't tell me what I doubt. Like I said, you don't know me."

[I know *all* men as I know myself. We are one.]

Dylan rubbed a hand over his face, buying himself a breath. Pathmaker's certainty pressed on him harder than the night outside.

"Usually, when I step into a situation, I bring grace. Hope, maybe. I save lives or at least inspire something…better." Dylan exhaled shakily. "I thought that was the point of all this."

[*You* do this work? Or someone does it through you?]

Dylan met the warrior's steady gaze and said nothing.

[Your young eyes see beyond the moment?]

"Sometimes."

[Every moment?]

Dylan shook his head.

[Does the Lone Man—by whatever name *you* call Him—see every moment?]

A muscle ticked in Dylan's cheek. He hated the question—not because he doubted, but because he needed the answer to be true tonight more than ever.

"I…I believe He does. Yeah."

[Then perhaps He sees what you cannot. Knows what you cannot.]

Pathmaker studied him a long moment, eyes steady, unblinking.

[The beast casts its fog to sever prey from the world, to blind them to anything but fear and despair.]

He tapped his chest lightly, but with meaning.

[You breathe that same fog now. Grief. Anger. Doubt. It clouds your vision more than the mist outside. And if you cannot see clearly, young one, you risk walking us all into the creature's jaws.]

Dylan's breath hitched—a subtle wince, as

if the warrior had pressed a thumb into a bruise he'd been pretending wasn't there.

Pathmaker continued, his voice low and steady.

[When my father took me on my first hunt, I killed a deer. I foolishly believed I had won the respect of my tribe. I imagined their praise, my mother's pride, the feast we would share. But in my rush for glory, I had killed a breeding doe. My people do not do this. It is forbidden.

My imaginings were folly. My father chastised me for being quick to kill and slow to think. I had seen only what I wanted to be true, not what was.]

He leaned forward slightly.

[If the One you serve is good and just, would He allow such a fate for the girl if it were not necessary?]

Dylan's eyes shut briefly. "You've made your point."

[Perhaps, at the end of all days, her sacrifice will be understood. Among my people, to die in service to the tribe is honorable. Worthy of celebration. The Lone Man rewards such bravery in the afterlife.]

"I said you made your point," Dylan repeated, softer now. "It's not that I doubt. It's that faith isn't the antidote for pain."

[No. But it *is* a balm. Our pain is soothed by knowing it will not last forever.]

Dylan nodded, breath steadying as he rose from the chair.

Pathmaker studied him.

[Is there a reason you hide the truth from them?]

"About what?"

[Where I came from.]

"There's no reason. It just…isn't what matters right now."

The warrior tilted his head.

[You are a strange man.]

Dylan huffed a humorless breath. "You're not the first to say so."

He left the kitchen without another word. He approached Captain Meeks slowly, making enough noise on the floorboards that he wouldn't startle the man.

"Anything?" Dylan asked.

"Hard to say," Meeks replied, eyes fixed on the fog. "That mess out there is a hole in my radar—keeps me blind until something's damn near breathing on us. Still no bogies. But after everything tonight?" He tapped his temple. "I trust my gut more than my eyes."

"And what's your gut say?"

"That we're being watched," Meeks said. "That the bastard's out there, waiting for us to make the next move."

Dylan nodded, jaw tight.

"Hey, kid," Meeks added after a moment, "I'm sorry about the girl. I know you said you haven't been here long, but…that's a bad beat. You sure she's, uh—"

"I'm sure."

Meeks let the silence stretch. "If there's even a chance…well, I don't believe in leaving a man behind."

"She's dead, Captain."

Meeks exhaled through his nose, still scanning the fog, rifle steady.

"Yeah," he said quietly. "I figured."

He adjusted his grip on the rifle, the motion practiced, automatic.

"So the plan, as I understand it," he continued, "is to follow our native friend through the soup. But to where?"

"Safety," Dylan said. "Not your home. Not yet. Not Pathmaker's cither. Somewhere *else*—somewhere Ollie saw in her vision."

"And how's this Pathmaker fella supposed to know where that is?"

"I couldn't say," Dylan admitted. "But… that's the story as Ollie saw it."

"And you don't think she could be wrong?"

"No," Dylan said quietly. "I don't. I'm sorry. I know you'd like more than that."

"Kid," Meeks said, "I was flying over the Atlantic, hit a hole in the sky, crashed into nothing, and ended up in Civil War Georgia during year nine of a four-year war. Nothing about my day makes sense. But you've got grit, and my gut says you're the one seeing the big picture. So, if trusting somebody to lead us out of here is the play, you're my guy. We go where you say."

"Thank you, Captain."

"Heard you squawking with our tattooed friend in there. Seemed tense."

"It's fine," Dylan said.

"Didn't *seem* fine."

Dylan set his face and said nothing.

"It's okay, kid," Meeks said. "You don't owe me the details. Just making sure we're all on board with the plan."

"We are," Dylan said. "And, Captain...I suspect we'll cross paths with that thing on the way."

"That's not what you told the Beaumont kids."

"No," Dylan replied. "It's not."

The pilot studied him for a beat—recognition flickering there. *Need-to-know.* He'd lived his whole career on that principle. And Dylan hadn't handed him classified information out of arrogance...but out of trust.

"Alright," Meeks said quietly. "So if we *do* run into it?"

"I aim to kill it."

Meeks turned to study him. Really study him.

"You honestly think we can? Something big enough and strong enough to tear down a wall like it was tin foil?"

"I've fought tougher," Dylan said, flat and certain. "And I'm still kicking."

Meeks huffed a half-laugh. "Good on you, kid. Personally, I'm a little scared. Ain't no shame in it long as we finish the job."

"I'm not the one that ought to be frightened," Dylan said.

Meeks gave a thin smile and turned back to the fog.

"Roger that."

When George returned with his pack and the large carpet bag Elizabeth had loaded, his sister followed close behind with a shotgun in her hands. Pathmaker, finished sharpening his axe and the knife at his belt, drifted in after them.

"Trade me," Elizabeth said, offering the shotgun to Captain Meeks. He handed her the Henry in return.

"It's loaded," she added.

Meeks nodded. "And reloading?"

"You'll die before you finish it," George said dryly.

"Roger that," Meeks muttered.

"Pathmaker will take the lead," Dylan said. "Elizabeth directly behind him. I'll carry her bag and follow her. George behind me with his pack, and Captain Meeks will bring up the rear. Don't lose sight of the person in front of you—no more than three steps back or the fog will swallow you. If they stop, you stop. And no talking. Just because you can't see the monster doesn't mean it won't hear you."

As Dylan spoke, George crossed to a water-stained wooden trunk in the corner. He lifted a long roll of white linen and brought it over.

"George?"

"You should carry this," George said, unwrapping the bundle to reveal a saber. "It was my father's. They returned it to us when…well. You know."

Dylan laughed—sudden, unexpected—and all four companions jolted.

Meeks, eyes still on the breach in the wall, said, "What the hell's funny, kid?"

"I'd like to know as well," Elizabeth said.

Dylan took the saber by the hilt and shook his head. "Ollie. She told me a few things about what would happen tonight—after she was taken. She said I'd look like quite the hero with the Captain's pistol in one hand and a sword in the other. But with everything else she told me, it didn't really sink in. I just asked for the pistol and forgot the rest."

"You did say the sword was your weapon of choice," Meeks replied.

"That I did," Dylan said. "Thank you, George. I'll handle it with care."

"It doesn't matter," George said. "If it keeps you safe…or one of us…it's worth it."

[It is a good gift,] Pathmaker said. [Destined, I think, for this hunt.]

"What did he say?" Elizabeth asked.

"He likes it," Dylan said. "Very shiny."

"When do we leave?" George asked.

"Now," Dylan said. "Your leg gonna hold up?"

"It'll have to."

Dylan nodded, then turned to Elizabeth.

"Elizabeth, do you have any experience with that rifle? Other than threatening me with it, I mean?"

She flushed. "I'm sorry for that. And no, I've never fired it. George should take it."

She handed it over. George slid the Henry into his pack, tested the draw, and nodded once.

"Pathmaker," Dylan said. "It's time."

The warrior stepped past them and dropped cleanly through the torn side of Beaumont House, landing with the graceful confidence of someone born to the hunt. He waited below, arms ready.

Elizabeth paused at the shattered edge—one final glance back at the home she'd grown up in—then took Dylan's hand and eased herself down into Pathmaker's waiting arms. He set her gently on her feet and turned his gaze toward the mist.

Dylan hopped down next, pivoting to help George manage the drop. Captain Meeks followed, landing with practiced surefootedness despite the shotgun in hand.

Once all were gathered, Pathmaker moved forward into the fog, and the hesitant band of travelers fell in behind him.

B y the time Pathmaker guided them past the twin jacarandas marking the front of the Beaumont estate, George was already winded and struggling to keep pace. The warrior sensed it and stopped, raising a hand to halt the line behind him.

"We can't stay long," Dylan whispered. "The fog slows *us*—not the beast. Standing still just makes us easier prey."

George nodded, motioning for them to continue even as his breath came hard.

Elizabeth said nothing. Instead, she stepped back to him, kissed his cheek, and offered a brave smile.

He returned one of his own—thin, but genuine—trying to assure her he was alright.

Dylan pointed ahead so Elizabeth would notice Pathmaker had resumed moving. She hurried to catch up, and George fell in behind her. Dylan glanced back at Meeks, who gave him a steady, confident nod, shotgun at the ready.

Together, the little band pressed on into the pale murk.

From time to time, through the muted hiss of wind, they heard branches snapping or the low, rolling rumble of a distant growl. Each sound came from just far enough away to offer a fragile illusion of safety.

To the Beaumont siblings, the landscape felt almost foreign. Only the occasional land-mark stirred a fuzzy memory—an echo of a world that had once made sense. The long war had devoured the country, its people, its re-sources. Families were scattered. Homes looted or burned. For every Union victory, the Confederacy clawed back more ground somewhere else, and the civilians trapped between them paid the price as the years dragged on.

Half a mile from their front door, the neighbors' home stood in ruin—a charred mockery of its former elegance. Blackened rafters jutted like broken ribs through the overgrowth, and where laughter and hymn-singing had once filled its halls, only the scritch-scratching of rats and raccoons remained.

Elizabeth wondered what had become of the Martin family. Had they died there in the only home they'd ever known, or abandoned it when the fighting inched too close? Many had fled, of course. But George had convinced her and Ollie to stay.

"Nowhere is safe," he had told them. "This war will consume us all before it's done. And the foolishness that sparked it will haunt us long after. We've stayed out of the conflict, and Father's ties on both sides bought us time. But the fight will come for us eventually. And if I must fall to this madness, I'd rather die at home."

Elizabeth and Ollie had agreed, not because they believed him entirely but, because they knew George could protect them better within the walls of Beaumont House than on any open road.

Pathmaker lifted a hand and stopped so abruptly that Elizabeth nearly ran into him. The others halted behind her as the warrior strode back to Dylan.

[We are being herded.]

"Explain," Dylan said.

[Because I do not know this land, I've chosen our direction based on where I sense our enemy is *not*. But it is clever. It has been circling us and driving us toward fewer options.]

"Do we fight?"

"Fight?" George repeated, alarmed.

[No. It will not strike here. I do not feel the tension before a kill. It is patient. We must remain the same…calm, steady…until our moment to turn on the predator comes.]

Dylan nodded.

"What did he say?" George asked. "What's this about a fight?"

"No fight," Dylan replied. "I just needed to know how close the danger is."

George stared at him. "Why do I feel like you aren't telling me everything?"

"Good instincts," Meeks said, stepping forward. "Look, Beaumont—the kid's got a plan. And sometimes a good plan means keeping folks in the dark until it's time. Less to overthink. Less to get killed over."

George grimaced but accepted it with a nod.

Dylan turned back to Pathmaker. "How do we proceed?"

[We keep moving until the path shows itself. If the creature attacks first, we fight—and pray the Lone Man is with us.]

Dylan exhaled. "As plans go, I'm not loving it."

[You asked me to lead, young one. I can only do what I can.]

"Then lead on," Dylan said. He glanced at George. "You okay?"

"I'll live," George answered. "Good Lord willing."

"If someone's offering prayers," Meeks muttered, "kindly add me to your list."

For what felt like hours, Pathmaker led them through the murk with the confidence of a man following a known trail. Only he and Dylan understood the truth—he was guiding them by instinct alone, instincts honed across more hunts than he could name.

Of their two goals—getting the Beaumont siblings to safety and ending the beast before it destroyed anyone else—Pathmaker leaned toward the latter. If he found a portal to deliver George and Elizabeth to safety, the soldier called Meeks would escort them through while he and Dylan carried the hunt onward. He prayed silently that the Lone Man and the spirits of his ancestors would guide him to a place where he could both protect *and* fight.

Pathmaker did not trouble himself with

how much the others knew. The hunt had already cost him a season of his life—months spent following tracks no one else could read after the creature tore through his people and vanished into the murk. He had never laid eyes on the beast's true form, but he knew the way it stalked its prey…and the grim joy it seemed to take in the kill.

They had just crossed the road into what remained of a once-thriving cotton patch—burned, trampled, left for dead by marching armies—when a faint sound reached Pathmaker's ear. He raised his hand, halting the group.

Dylan heard it too. He lifted Meeks's pistol toward the mist.

The captain slid closer, shotgun leveled. "Bogey?"

"It's toying with us," Dylan whispered.

George pulled the Henry from his pack. "We're out in the open here. We need cover. Doc Horton's place should be close…just south of here past that copse of trees, I think."

"No offense, George," Meeks muttered, eyes scanning the fog, "but if this beasty tore open *your* house, there ain't a wall in Georgia that's gonna keep it out."

"He's right," Dylan said, motioning Pathmaker over. When the warrior approached, Dylan added quietly, "I'm going to split off. If I can't draw the thing away, I'll flank it. That way, if it moves on you, I can hit it hard."

"Now hold on," Meeks said.

[It is a mighty hunter,] Pathmaker warned. [You cannot sneak up on it.]

"I know neither of you really knows me," Dylan replied, "but I'm not like anyone else in this story."

[You believe you can slay the creature alone?]

Dylan smiled faintly. "I've got something better than skill, my friend. I have authority. And a sword. Don't worry, there'll be more than enough vengeance to share."

"Ollie told you this," George said quietly. "She said you'd leave us."

"Only for a little while," Dylan answered. "I made her a promise, and I intend to keep it."

"This whole trek feels FUBAR, kid," Meeks muttered. "And I don't like you out there solo."

"That," Dylan said, "and I'm taking your pistol with me."

"Well, yeah. That too."

"I said I'd give it back, Captain. I'm a man of my word."

Pathmaker bowed his head.

[The Lone Man walks with you. May He lead you to victory.]

"And lead you to safety," Dylan replied.

"What did he say?" George asked.

"He was wishing me luck," Dylan said. He turned to Elizabeth. "Stick to your brother like glue, Elizabeth. And if that thing comes for you, don't panic. Stories often look darkest right before the light breaks through. Keep moving. Keep trusting. The Author is at work for our good."

"Dylan?" she said softly.

"Yes?"

"Call me Lizzie."

The kindness in her voice made him smile. "Thank you, Lizzie."

They watched him vanish into the mist—first a silhouette, then a shadow, then nothing at all.

And with their hearts pounding and a warrior they barely understood leading them forward, the others continued into the waiting night.

Pathmaker could feel the monster on their heels, its keen eyes tracking their every step. The murky night belonged to the creature; it held every advantage. Yet deep within him, deeper than instinct or the lessons of his people, Pathmaker felt the Lone Man at work. Greater hands were moving the story forward. Hope lived, and he would track that hope as surely as he tracked all things.

Behind him, Lizzie fought the uneven ground and kept her silence. She forced her mind away from Ollie, saving grief for later—if later ever came. Every few steps she glanced back to be certain George remained upright. She could only imagine the agony in his leg.

George limped forward, leaving Beaumont House to the creeping fog. The loss stung—but not like the thought of Ollie, dying scared and alone while he and Lizzie were powerless to reach her.

Lizzie needs you now, his mind repeated like prayer. *Keep moving.*

He had become master of Beaumont House long before he'd felt ready: eighteen years old, parents gone, two little sisters depending on him. He'd stepped into the role he never wanted because the alternative was losing them. They had survived that storm…until the brume brought a new one.

At the rear, Captain Meeks moved with shotgun raised, nerves sharp. In a cockpit, radar would have told him where the threat hid. Here, he felt blind—like a kite going up against a MiG-29. Outmatched. Outgunned. Only the kid, Dylan, kept him steady. Whatever was coming, Meeks intended to meet it fighting.

When George stopped suddenly, Meeks froze and brought the shotgun up.

"See something, George?" he whispered.

"Keep your voice down. Pathmaker signaled Lizzie to stop."

Before Meeks could respond, Lizzie slapped a trembling hand over her mouth, muffling a scream. Her other hand shot out, pointing into the mist.

George and Meeks squinted into the swirl of white. George drew the Henry from his pack and sighted down its barrel. A shape emerged—small, familiar.

His breath caught. His arms sagged.

Olivia Beaumont was walking toward them through the fog.

***

[T]his is a trick,] Pathmaker said. [A lure. Nothing more.]

"Ollie?" Lizzie breathed, taking a hesitant step forward.

"Lizzie," George warned. "Dylan told us—"

"You don't have to be afraid, George," Olivia said, her voice calm, almost gentle.

"We watched it take you," George replied. "We have *every* reason to be afraid."

"Yeah, I'm not loving this," Meeks muttered, keeping the shotgun trained on her. "What's my effective range here if this turns ugly?"

"Put that thing down," Lizzie hissed. "It's Ollie." Then, remembering Dylan's warning, added, "Isn't it?"

Olivia limped toward them, bruised, hair mussed.

"I tricked it," she said. "It chased after Dylan. When it left me alone, I ran to find you."

[Do not trust this,] Pathmaker said, low and urgent.

"I may not speak Cherokee or whatever our pal's speaking," Meeks whispered, "but that tone's telling me we pump the brakes. She got any way to…prove herself?"

"Ollie," George said, raising a hand, "before you come any closer, tell us something only *you* would know."

"George, I'm hurt," she said. "And that monster could come back any moment."

"Then prove it," he snapped. "Now."

"George!" Lizzie protested, swatting his arm. "You've known Dylan barely a day and Ollie her whole life!"

"George just wants to keep us safe," Olivia said soothingly. "Like when he punched mean old Martin Tolliver square in his crooked jaw. Martin wanted to *breed* our sweet sister, and George taught him better."

Lizzie recoiled. "Breed?" The word felt rotten in her mouth.

"Martin shot you," Olivia continued, eyes fixed on George, "because he was too cowardly to take the beating he had earned."

Pathmaker stepped between them.

[Do not be deceived, friends. Your sister is dead. Our enemy toys with your hearts.]

"I'm calling bullshit on all this," Meeks said. "If she takes another step, she's getting both barrels."

"That's my *sister!*" George hissed. Then

louder: "Ollie! Did you see where Dylan went after he left us?"

"No," she answered, limping closer. "But we can't trust him, George. He lied about my visions. He told me if I ran, the beast would kill you and Lizzie. But right before I was taken, I had a vision. Dylan's working with that thing. A devil in our midst."

"George," Lizzie whispered. "I'm not so sure now. I'm scared."

"Don't be," a voice called from the fog.

Dylan Drake stepped into the clearing between them, calm but deadly serious. "She's got a convincing story," he said. "And she's right… you don't know me well enough to dismiss it without consideration. But she's made a mistake that's going to cost her."

Olivia smiled—a smile that wasn't Olivia Beaumont's.

"Don't listen to him, George. He's not what he pretends to be."

George swallowed hard. "What mistake, Dylan?"

Dylan raised Captain Meek's pistol. His

voice shook, not with fear, but with fury. "She's wearing the face of someone I cared for. And that pisses me off."

The gunshot cracked through the fog, precise as Dylan intended. The bullet punched cleanly through the bridge of Olivia's nose, sending a fine red mist into the air.

Lizzie screamed. Meeks lowered his shotgun in shock. Pathmaker surged past him toward Dylan, shouting something urgent in his own tongue.

Lizzie collapsed against her brother, sobbing into his shoulder. He shook her hard—harder than he liked—to drag her back to the present.

"Lizzie, look!"

She blinked through tears and lifted her head.

What stood before them was Olivia in shape only. A neat, dime-sized hole sat dead center between her eyes, but instead of blood, blue ichor trickled down her cheek. And she was smiling. Smiling in a way no human mouth should.

"I lost you in the mist," the thing said, its

voice almost—but not quite—Olivia's. Its gaze slid over Dylan. "What *are* you, boy?"

"An enemy you'll wish you hadn't made," Dylan replied. "Pathmaker!"

The warrior was already in motion. While still sprinting, he hurled his axe. It struck the false Olivia in the shoulder, slicing downward at a grotesque angle until it lodged deep near the abdomen.

Dylan opened fire. With each hit, the illusion buckled until the entire form burst outward, collapsing into writhing segments. What had seemed to be a girl's body was only the articulated tip of a much larger appendage—head and torso one probing digit, the limbs merely others.

The shattered pieces slithered away, revealing the monstrous truth behind them:

A giant, many-jointed hand, unfurling from the fog like a nightmare made flesh.

Meeks thumbed back both hammers on the shotgun, but George grabbed his arm.

"You'll hit Dylan or Pathmaker," George warned, "*if* the shot even reaches."

"Damn." Meeks pulled the weapon tight against his chest and sprinted toward the fight.

George set his feet, raised the Henry, found the largest part of the exposed hand—and fired.

T he hand of the beast—vast, jointed, and shedding the last semblance of Olivia Beaumont's form—swung at them with a speed that mocked its impossible size. Dylan moved first, slipping beneath the blow with an agility that startled even Pathmaker. He dodged a second swipe with a fluid twist of his torso.

Captain Meeks wasn't so lucky.

Two thick fingers caught him mid-stride and hoisted him into the air before he could even fire. His breath left him in a grunt of surprise—

—and then an axe whirled upward in a perfect arc.

The blade struck the digit holding him, severing it just above the knuckle. Meeks dropped like a stone, landing hard on his shoulder. As he groaned, the monstrous hand recoiled, retreating into the mist with a chorus of guttural snarls. It circled them just beyond sight, its growls vibrating through the ground.

"It isn't done," Dylan said, decocking the pilot's pistol and tossing it back to him. "Weapons up. Eyes open."

Lizzie and George hurried to join them, hands clasped.

"You knew it wasn't her," she said, voice trembling.

"So did you, Lizzie," George reminded. "How?"

"The way she spoke of Martin," Lizzie whispered, trembling. "As if it were nothing. As if that day hadn't shattered *everything*."

She swallowed hard.

"Our Ollie would *never* have used such a cruel word—not about me, not about *anyone*. She knew what that night cost us. She'd die before she threw that hurt in my face."

Pathmaker moved to Dylan's side, eyes scanning the fog.

[We take our stand here. It will come before

morning. And in this clearing, we will see its approach.]

Dylan nodded.

"I'm sorry, Lizzie," he said. "I know you wanted to believe. I just couldn't let that thing get to you or George. I made Ollie a promise… and I mean to keep it."

"How quickly I doubted you when given half a reason," she hugged him, then looked him in the eye. "I don't deserve your forgiveness, but I'll ask for it all the same."

"Nothing to forgive." Dylan glanced to George. "You alright?"

George swallowed hard and shook his head.

"Take a moment," Dylan said. "It may be all we get. Captain?"

Meeks rubbed his shoulder, winced, and rolled it experimentally.

"Bruised and embarrassed, kid, but still mission-capable. What's the plan?"

"Shoot anything that comes through the fog," Dylan replied, "and try not to die doing it."

Pathmaker hefted his axe.

[It would be a noble death.]

"What'd he say?" Meeks asked.

Dylan glanced at Pathmaker's axe. "He's… very motivated."

"I suspect your translating ain't exactly five-by-five, kid," Meeks said, handing Lizzie the shotgun she had loaned him. "Given the size of that hand, we seem a tad outmatched. You don't happen to have an Abrams on you, I suppose?"

"Fresh out of tanks," Dylan said with a chuckle. "But we don't need one. Morning is coming soon and we've wounded it."

"Maybe it'll get sloppy," Meeks said, nodding. "Show us its belly."

"We can't survive on a maybe," George replied, ramming cartridges into the Henry. "What happened to getting us away from it?"

"Where would we go, George?" Lizzie asked. "Even if we found a portal, what would stop it from following us through?"

"The kid's right," Meeks added. "My world's got enough worries without importing a shapeshifting nightmare. I'd sooner die than drag that trouble back to '95."

"And even if we escaped," Lizzie whispered, "we would leave *our* world to be devoured. I won't let it do to anyone else what it did to Ollie."

George nodded once, grim and resigned.

Dylan hesitated. "There's something I haven't told you about Pathmaker. Until now, it didn't matter."

"Spill it, kid," Meeks said.

Pathmaker's expression hardened.

[They will not believe you.]

"It doesn't matter," Dylan replied. "Pathmaker isn't from the past, but an altered future. His world reached the modern age—just without colonization. His people never abandoned who they were."

"How?" Meeks frowned. "If it wasn't England, it would've been Spain. Or the French."

"In *his* reality, no empire grew large enough to attempt it," Dylan said. "Nations stayed small. Grew inward. And by the time anyone thought to expand, colonization was seen as barbaric. Europeans came as traders, not pilgrims. The tribes on this continent flourished, united, powerful, and eventually became a world power in their own right."

Lizzie folded her arms. "And what does that have to do with the creature hunting us?"

"Everything," Dylan answered. "Pathmaker's world was at war too—tribes divided by outside manipulation. In that conflict the beast appeared. It fed on the chaos."

George looked at Pathmaker, eyes wide. "You're telling me he *knows* this thing?"

"He hunted it," Dylan said quietly. "He and his warriors tracked it after it annihilated an entire village in the land you know as Virginia. It attacked him and dragged him through the tear into this world, which is when you found him."

"My world," Meeks said, "was nearly swept into a mess in Vietnam. We stayed out of it, but that country's still tearing itself apart. Death toll's unreal. And the fighting here's been going on nine damn years? That *can't* be a coincidence."

Pathmaker's eyes narrowed.

[The demon feeds on conflict. Its sustenance is chaos and pain, hatred and violence.]

"In my world," Dylan added, "the United States *did* get involved in Vietnam, Captain Meeks. And it cost us lives…and in other ways we'll never tally. I think whoever opened these portals dragged the beast to places where war was already doing the heavy lifting."

Lizzie drew a sharp breath. "Who would *do* such a thing?"

"Someone powerful," Dylan said. "Someone who hates the Author and everything He intends. But Pathmaker knows this monster. Understands how it hunts, how it thinks."

"A tactical advantage," Meeks said, "so long as he shares his intel with the rest of the squad."

"Pathmaker?" Dylan prompted.

The warrior stepped closer to the group.

[Though it wears many skins, its mass remains fixed. The larger the form, the weaker the creature. When it comes again, it will be small and quick as the wind. Vicious and harder to kill.]

The others looked to Dylan for translation.

"It's previous bulk was all about intimidation," Dylan said. "That size works against it. The smaller it gets, the worse it is—faster, nastier, and a lot harder to put down."

George nodded grimly. "We wounded it because it was a large, slow target. It won't make the same mistake twice."

"No," Dylan agreed. "It won't. That's why you and Lizzie need to stay tight with Captain Meeks. Pathmaker and I may need you, but… strike from a distance, hm?"

"I won't risk hitting either of you," Meeks said. "Told you, kid…I'm not that good a shot."

"I trust you," Dylan replied. "And George is solid with his Henry."

Lizzie lifted her chin. "And me?"

"George and Captain Meeks'll be watching their sights, waiting for an opening," Dylan said. "You're the guardrail. If that thing moves for them, Lizzie, you and the shotgun put a hole in it big enough to reconsider its life choices."

She nodded, jaw set.

"Any questions?" he asked.

"Yeah," Meeks said. "How do I get home if something happens to you?"

Dylan huffed a breath that wanted to be a laugh.

"Don't lose sleep over me, Captain. Ollie told me what to do. I just need to keep that thing busy until the right moment."

"This still ain't my idea of a plan," Meeks muttered, "but it seems to be all we've got."

"God will be with us," Lizzie said, the hope in her voice drawing their eyes to her.

"Hear, hear," George murmured.

Pathmaker rested a palm on his axe.

[May the Lone Man guide our weapons.]

Dylan nodded, steady. "Amen."

"Amen," Meeks echoed, racking the slide on his Sig. "And pass the ammunition."

Dylan and Captain Meeks kept watch while Pathmaker gathered wood and built a fire. Lizzie, still shaken from seeing the monster wear her sister's face, hummed a familiar hymn under her breath. George held her close, rubbing her arm to keep her warm and steady her nerves.

"Our friend seemed pretty intent on getting a fire going," Meeks said. "Think it'll keep the beasty at bay?"

"Pathmaker," Dylan asked, "is the creature afraid of fire?"

[No.]

"Then why build one?"

[I am cold. If we must wait, I prefer warmth.]

"What'd he say?" Meeks asked.

"He was cold," Dylan muttered.

Meeks laughed—short, sharp, and involuntary. It startled everyone, even him.

"Sorry. Needed that."

Before Dylan could answer, George tensed. "Dylan?"

The concern in his voice pulled every eye

toward the edge of the fog. About twenty yards away, a mountain lion stepped out of the murk—head low, muscles taut, eyes locked on the people around the fire.

"Pathmaker?" Dylan asked. "Is that it?"

[Perhaps.]

"That's… not helpful."

[It can wear many faces, young one. It is best we assume the worst.]

George already had the Henry raised. "If it moves, I've got it."

"No," Dylan said, stepping forward. "It could just be an animal driven here by a much larger predator."

"Or pushed out by war," George agreed. "Still, if it charges—"

"Monster or not," Lizzie whispered, "I'd rather it not get any closer."

Dylan nodded. "Let me handle it. If it *is* the creature, you all know what to do."

They watched him cross the clearing alone. The lion hissed, growled, then coiled to leap. Dylan lifted both palms and spoke, firm and low, words none of the others could make out.

The lion's ears flattened. Its growl softened to a pur. Then slowly it lifted its head, turned, and trotted back into the fog.

When Dylan returned to the fire and warmed his hands, the others simply stared.

"What the hell was that?" Meeks asked.

"I told him we meant no harm," Dylan said.

"And it just listened? Because you're so damn scary?" Meeks asked.

"No, Captain. It wasn't intimidation that made him listen. It was authority."

"Right," Meeks muttered, shaking his head. "Authority. Naturally."

Pathmaker tilted his head, studying him.

[Who are you, that you speak to the beasts? More than a boy. The Lone Man's mark is surely on you.]

"The Author makes the rules," Dylan replied. "Even a mountain lion knows when it's outmatched."

"You're a real piece of work, kid," Meeks said with a smirk. "The boys on the Truman would never believe the set of—look! There!"

All eyes followed his outstretched arm.

A wolf stepped from the fog, if wolf was still the right word. It stood twice the size of any natural creature, its eyes burning with electric-blue light. Sparks cracked off its pupils like embers from a forge.

Pathmaker's spun his axe in the palm of his hand.

[Do not let this form fool you. It can alter it with little more than a thought.]

"Don't believe what you see," Dylan relayed to the others. "It shifted once; it can do it again."

"Copy that," Meeks said, peeling off to the left, pistol raised. Pathmaker mirrored him to the right, flanking instinctively.

"George," Dylan said, "you've got the most range with that Henry. Move back with Lizzie. If you get a clear shot, take it. Lizzie, if it closes the distance, your shotgun will matter more than the rifle. Make it count."

Lizzie swallowed and nodded. George steadied her with a hand on her back.

"And you?" Lizzie asked, voice tight, eyes flicking from the wolf to Dylan.

Dylan gave her a small, tired smile—grief, resolve, and something older flickering behind his eyes.

"I'm gonna go make this personal."

***

The wolf ignored the native warrior and the navy pilot. Its glowing blue eyes locked onto the young man sprinting toward it with a saber in hand.

It crouched low, ready to meet his charge—only for Dylan to drop suddenly into a slide, vanishing beneath its jaws at the exact moment it leapt.

A gunshot cracked from the rear of the clearing.

The creature's left eye burst in a shower of blue fire.

Reeling, the wolf twisted just as Dylan's sliding momentum carried him beneath its ribs. His saber drove upward, deep into its belly. The beast shrieked, kicked him away like a doll, and wheeled toward the man who had taken its eye.

As it charged, its body convulsed violently. Fur thickened. Its frame expanded. Mid-stride the wolf melted into a massive grizzly bear, each pounding step rattling the earth.

Gunfire erupted. Bullets tore through fur and flesh, but the beast barreled on.

Wounded and enraged, it lashed out, swiping its massive paw at one of the armed men, ripping his flesh from his shoulder down to his belly.

Pathmaker buried his axe deep into the bear's flank at the exact moment its claws tore through him. Pain blinded him. He never saw the beast lower its massive head to finish the kill—nor the blur of Dylan, swift as lightning, bringing the borrowed saber across the creature's neck in a near-decapitating arc.

Somewhere beyond the warrior's fading vision, Captain Meeks cursed and charged in, each gunshot cracking through the night as he tried to draw the monster's attention. But Pathmaker saw none of it. Death pressed close.

"Hang on, my friend!" Dylan's voice strained through the roaring in his ears. "Today is *not* the day you meet your ancestors. Fight! We need you!"

At the sound of Dylan's voice, Pathmaker's sight flickered back. The bear reared and swiped at the navy pilot, who barely rolled clear. Dylan —fearless, furious—leapt higher than Pathmaker believed a human could and aimed again for the creature's throat.

But midleap, the beast changed.

Dylan's blade met only air as the bear collapsed inward, its form contorting and hardening. The boy fell awkwardly, landing hard, breath smashed from his lungs. In the bear's place rose a scorpion the same size the bear had been, claws snapping, tail arched to strike.

It surged toward the Beaumont siblings.

Only George's precise shooting slowed it, blue ichor spraying with each hit. The brief hesitation gave Dylan the seconds he needed to scramble to the fallen warrior.

"Boss," Dylan breathed, hands slick with Pathmaker's blood, "You've healed him once… same as You did the captain. You didn't bring him this far to let him die here."

His exhaustion bled through the words.

"I'm too small for this. You'll have to do what I can't."

He wiped a tear away with the cuff of his sleeve.

"Please."

The thunder of Lizzie's shotgun ripped him back to the moment.

The creature had realized George's Henry was doing the most damage and wheeled toward him, stinger poised to punch through his heart. Lizzie's shot, however, made it reconsider. Buckshot shattered one of its pincers, spraying blue gore across the dirt.

She didn't have time to reload. Dylan knew it.

He closed the distance in a blur and brought the saber down hard, severing the scorpion's tail at the second segment. The beast screeched, spun—

—and shifted again.

Its body swelled, thickened, hardened. In seconds, a rhinoceros—an animal the Beaumonts had only ever seen in illustrations—stood pawing at the earth, snorting steam into the cold night.

Captain Meeks watched in horror as the horned monster barreled into Dylan. The impact sounded like a battering ram slamming into a wall. Dylan flew backward, skidding across the ground as Meeks reloaded and fired to draw the creature's attention, anything to buy the Beaumonts a few steps of distance from the thing that had murdered their sister.

Behind him, Pathmaker stirred.

[The Lone Man has spoken,] he rasped.

Meeks didn't understand the words, but he heard the urgency. He kept firing.

Pathmaker tried again, forcing the English his mother had once taught him. "Weak," he gasped. "Weak…when change."

Meeks hesitated only a heartbeat. "What?"

"Weak…when change," the warrior repeated, voice trembling. "Boy need know. Weak when change."

Meeks looked down at the wounded warrior, trying to make sense of the strained words. When he lifted his gaze again, a rhinoceros was already thundering toward him. The ground shook with each step.

With only seconds to react, he raised his pistol and fired—praying more than aiming. Against all odds, the bullet drove straight into the creature's eye. The rhino bellowed and stumbled, veering just enough for Meeks to dive clear of its horn.

"Weak when…change," Pathmaker rasped again.

"Kid!" Meeks shouted. "Our Indian pal says it's weak when it changes!"

The creature heard him.

It convulsed mid-stride, its bulk collapsing inward, bones rearranging in a grotesque fluidity. In an instant, the rhinoceros was gone.

A man stood in its place.

Tall, lean, muscular. Skin smoothing as if

poured over a frame still deciding on a shape. The ruined hollows of its face sealed and darkened, eyes blooming back into place as though they had never been gone.

It smiled—too wide, too knowing—and bent to pick up Pathmaker's fallen axe.

"Your friend is very clever," it said, turning the blade casually in its hand. "But I won't need to change again. I have taken the form of the most dangerous animal on this world."

Dylan, still catching his breath, staggered to his feet. "Yeah, well…we're a messy bunch. Rageful and obstinate. Slow to think, quick to act." He wiped blood from his lip with the back of his hand. "But we've got something going for us that you don't."

The thing raked its tongue across its teeth. "Please. Enlighten me."

"We were created in the image of our Maker," Dylan said, lifting the saber, "and given authority over all creation. This world is ours. But you…you don't belong here. You're an abomination."

It snorted at that.

"Your ending was written in indelible ink long before you slithered into this world," Dylan said. "Simply put—you're *already* dead. You just don't know it yet."

The beast's human lips peeled into something meant to resemble a smile.

"You believe your creator reigns supreme. Yet I was sent here by another of great power. Either he could not stop her...or he has permitted me to kill."

"You've got free will," Dylan replied. "You can do as much evil as you can squeeze into your miserable existence. But I've got the will to stop you...and the authority to boot. You wanna fight destiny? Fine. You fight *me.*"

The creature tilted its head.

"Have you asked yourself why your creator did not warn you of the girl's death?"

It took a deep breath as if savoring the moment.

"Or why he let you fail her... just as you will fail these fragile things?"

Dylan's grip faltered—a heartbeat, nothing

more—but the wound landed. He steadied himself, eyes narrowing.

"I believe He sees more than I do," Dylan said. "And *certainly* more than *you*."

It sneered. "He won't save you."

Dylan didn't flinch this time. "I believe He *can*. I hope He *will*. But even if He doesn't, I'll serve Him with everything I am." He stepped forward. "And whether it's me who ends you or someone else down the line, you *won't* win. Not in the end. So quit your stalling. Let's finish this."

"Your friends will interfere."

Dylan raised a hand. "Nobody fires! Let me handle this."

Around them, guns lowered.

The creature's eyes gleamed. "Once you are dead, boy, I will savor their deaths one by one...nice and slow."

Dylan shook his head, almost amused. "You monsters never change. You hurt us, sure. Frightened us for a beat. But by night's end, I'll be cleaning your blood off this saber. And you'll be just another box checked off my to-do list. I'm unimpressed."

The thing growled, human features bending around the sound.

"I will feast on your flesh, young fool."

Dylan planted his feet.

"*Yeah-yeah.* Do your worst."

As Dylan and the beast—now wearing the shape of a man—clashed in the clearing, Captain Meeks dragged the wounded Pathmaker toward the fire. He had no training in this kind of wound, nothing in his naval experience that prepared him for a man torn open by claws the size of scythes. He wasn't sure the tracker had any business still breathing.

Lizzie rushed to help, passing George the shotgun so she could get her arms under Pathmaker's shoulders.

"Dear Lord," she whispered, "how is this poor man still alive?"

"Made of sterner stuff," Meeks said,

grunting as they lowered the warrior beside the flames. "Not unlike the kid."

George stared toward the clearing. "What does he think he's doing out there? We were barely holding our ground when it was five against one."

"I ain't exactly religious, mister," Meeks said, checking his pistol and scanning the fog, "but that kid's got angels riding shotgun or something. Never seen anybody move like that. And the hit he took from that rhino-thing? Should've killed him three times over. All this crazy is *way* above my pay grade but, if I had to put money down on this scrap, I'm betting the mortgage on the kid."

Pathmaker strained. "Weak—"

"Yeah, man, I told him," Meeks said quickly. "He heard you. Rest easy. The kid's got this."

Lizzie's voice trembled. "Where…where did they go?"

All three turned toward the clearing.

The fire cast its flickering glow on empty grass.

Boy and beast had vanished into the mist.

They couldn't see the fight, but they could hear it—the fierce ringing of saber and axe meeting again and again somewhere inside the brume, each clash echoing through the night like the tolling of iron bells.

Lizzie prayed silently.

George pressed his cheek to the Henry's stock, searching the fog for a target.

Meeks ripped open his survival vest, pulling free a morphine syringe and a battered first-aid kit.

"This'll take the edge off," he told Path-maker, plunging the needle into the warrior's arm. "Whatever mojo the kid pulled is knitting you back together, but I need you upright if things go south."

"Is that him?" George whispered.

A shape lurched out of the mist, dragging one leg behind it.

It wore Dylan's face—or what was left of it. Half the jaw hung loose, swinging with each step. Clothing slashed open, ribs visible beneath, the figure staggered as if pulled forward by invisible strings.

Meeks squared his shoulders, horror tightening his voice. "Kid?"

"I'm afraid your young friend didn't make it," the monster said, its borrowed human teeth too long, too sharp, too wrong. "I thought you should see what he looked like at the end."

"It's lying," Lizzie breathed.

Meeks raised his pistol. "And if he ain't?"

George's grip tightened on the Henry. For a heartbeat, none of them moved. The mist pressed close, swallowing sound, daring them to believe the worst. Grief hovered at the edges—raw, rising—ready to hollow them out if they let it.

"What hope do we have left?" George asked, finger whitening on the trigger.

"It's lying," Lizzie repeated, stronger now, fighting back the tremor in her voice. "That's what it is. A liar. A mockery of anything true. Dylan isn't dead."

"Whether he is or isn't," Meeks said, "I'm

not planning on dying polite. If this thing wants us, it's gonna work for it."

"Here, here," George muttered.

Lizzie took her brother's hand. "George, whatever happens…know that I love you. Ollie and I never expected you to be a father or mother. You were a boy asked to be a man far too soon."

"You girls were never burdens," George said thickly. "You are my sisters. Serving you both wasn't duty, Lizzie. It was love…and my honor."

"This is touching," Meeks cut in, shifting his grip on the Sig, "but my pal Pathmaker and I don't have anyone here to get sentimental over us. Maybe we focus on winning this damn thing?"

George nodded once.

"It was good to know you both," Lizzie said, offering each a smile and a nod.

"Back at ya, little miss," Meeks answered, never taking his eyes off the imposter.

[Wait.]

"How's that?" Meeks asked.

"Wait," Pathmaker rasped, forcing the word out.

"Wait for what?"

"Wait."

"I have a clear shot," George said. "Dead to rights, Captain."

"Wait," the warrior insisted again.

Meeks swallowed hard, kept his pistol trained on the creature wearing a friend's ruined face. Every instinct screamed to fire.

"Wait…wait…" Pathmaker murmured like a mantra—stronger each time, urgency rising.

"Something's moving in the fog," Lizzie whispered. "Something…fast."

"Now!" the warrior shouted.

George and Meeks fired in unison, bullets tearing through the creature's borrowed flesh. It staggered, holes blooming across its chest and shoulders.

"More!" Pathmaker barked, struggling upright. *[Force the change!]*

They obeyed, gunfire cracking through the night. The monster faltered, less than five yards away, its stolen features blurring, warping, and losing their shape as the bullets shredded its cohesion.

Then the thing stiffened. Its spine arched like a bowstring pulled to breaking.

"I grow tired of this," it hissed. Its body swelled, bones groaning, limbs stretching as something larger—far larger—fought to emerge. The air around it vibrated with a rising hum, the crackle of energy gathering for the shift.

One second more and it would be unstoppable.

A shadow burst from the fog.

Dylan hit the clearing at a dead sprint, saber catching the moonlight, his momentum carrying every ounce of force into a single upward arc. The blade met the creature midchange and sheared clean through its neck before the transformation could complete.

The head disintegrated first, unraveling into crackling blue energy. The half-changed body collapsed a beat later, dissolving as Dylan tumbled through it, hit the dirt hard, and rolled to a breathless stop.

He pushed to his feet, brushing off his sleeves as if nothing unusual had occurred.

"I was about to say the same thing," he said. "Everyone alright?"

"It said you were dead," George managed.

"It said a lot of things, George."

"How do we know it's really you?" Meeks asked.

"You tell me."

Meeks glanced at Pathmaker, helping the wounded warrior to his feet.

Pathmaker studied Dylan a moment, then nodded.

[It is he. The Lone Man's prophet.]

"I think that's Indian for 'everything's co-pacetic,'" Meeks said. "You had us worried, kid."

"It packed a wallop," Dylan said, staggering once before steadying himself. A gash along his forearm knit itself closed even as they watched, the blood drying faster than it should have. "Had me on the ropes for a minute or two, but the Boss had other plans."

George looked past them, squinting into the dark. "The mist has lifted."

It had—thinning in shreds, revealing the land all the way back toward Beaumont House.

[The shroud was the beast's doing,] Pathmaker said. [A veil it casts to cut its prey from the world, so no help may find them.]

He touched his chest, wincing.

[But you reached us. You broke its circle. This is the work of the Lone Man…or of one He has chosen. No ordinary man walks through a demon's fog and returns.]

"What was that?" Meeks asked.

"He said it's safe to head home," Dylan replied. "George, you set the pace."

"What about getting me home?" Meeks pressed. "Or our native friend here?"

"That'll happen, Captain. With the creature gone, any door will do. I can get you both back where you belong."

Meeks shook his head. "I've seen too much tonight to argue, kid, but I'm gonna have one helluva time processing this… vacation."

"Captain, please," Lizzie said sharply. "Your language."

Meeks blinked, chastened. "Sorry, little miss."

"Yes," George echoed. "Do watch your *damn* mouth in front of my sister."

Meeks shot him a bewildered look, as Dylan began laughing.

The others followed—relief mingled with exhaustion—while Pathmaker only smiled, steady and warm.

After saying their goodbyes, Dylan guided Captain Meeks and Pathmaker back to their own realities—places where their stories could continue without fear of the monster's shadow. Once they were safely home, he stepped through a waiting door in the Great Library and emerged from the cellar of Beaumont House, just as naturally as if he'd never left.

He stayed with George and Lizzie for several months. Together with a few surviving neighbors, they rebuilt the portion of the house the beast had torn away and repaired other areas long left to neglect. The work was grueling, but Dylan seemed to relish it—the rhythm of tools, the honest labor, the simple companionship of the Beaumonts.

As they worked, he noticed how the house itself seemed to breathe again. The tin roof—once warped and complaining—pinged softly in the afternoon heat like a creature remembering its voice.

Some evenings, Dylan tested the new porch boards the way George's grandfather once had —pressing his heel down just enough to hear the creak. The sound was different now, less mournful. The house no longer sagged beneath the weight of war and weather; it answered with a steadier voice. He would stand there and listen to the night. The fighting had moved farther north. The wrens were returning to nest in the oaks.

Once the last board was nailed and the final

stone set, they celebrated with a turkey dinner and a chocolate cake Lizzie baked from her mother's recipe. Afterward, they lingered by the fire with coffee in hand, letting the warmth settle around them.

Dylan was the first to break the silence.

"It's time for me to go."

George nodded slowly. "We knew the day would come, but…well, I dare say we've grown fond of having you around."

"Poor George only had sisters growing up," Lizzie said, refilling Dylan's cup. "You made him feel like he finally had a brother…and me, another."

"You two give me too much credit," Dylan said, a faint, wistful smile crossing his face. "But I'm grateful. More than I can say. These months…they've steadied me. Reminded me what it feels like to be rooted, even for a little while."

His smile faltered, touched by a sadness he didn't try to hide.

"But my path's already tugging at me again.

My part in your story is finished. Others need me now."

"We aren't so selfish as to keep your kindness from them," Lizzie offered. "When will you go?"

"Tonight."

"So soon?" George asked.

"It only takes the opening of a door, George. Or have you forgotten?"

Lizzie's eyes glimmered in the firelight. "Will we ever see you again?"

"After tonight? No. I'm afraid not. But you and George, and…Ollie will never be far from my thoughts."

"She was a bit sweet on you, our Ollie," Lizzie confessed. "She thought you were handsome. Mysterious. Then again, she understood you in ways we didn't."

"She was a kind soul," Dylan said. "And brave. You two were all she thought about. Even at the end…knowing what was coming for her."

George's gaze dropped to the flames. "We can rebuild this house…but there will always be a hole where our Ollie used to be. We can't fix that."

Dylan let the silence breathe before answering.

"No. You can't. But you'll heal. In time."

"How?" Lizzie whispered.

"By holding onto each other. By choosing love even when it hurts. The country is still at war…families breaking daily, hearts torn apart by miles or by principles. One day, hopefully soon, the fighting will end. For now, at least, it's moved north. Beaumont House is still standing."

George managed a small, weary smile. "A testament to my grandfather's design—and his stubbornness. It's the pride of our family."

"No. That's you and Lizzie, remember?" Dylan said. "This house—lovely and full of memories though it is—is still just a house."

George nodded, his smile warm if a bit sad.

"I'm afraid I need to ask a favor of you both," Dylan continued. "I'll understand if you can't oblige, but I have to ask all the same."

"We don't have much left," Lizzie said, "but

if it's in our power to help you, Dylan, we'd be happy to do it."

"The favor isn't for me," he said gently. "It's…um, for someone who can't ask you herself. There are other worlds out there, like the ones Captain Meeks and Pathmaker came from, places this monster hunted before it arrived here. Worlds torn apart by war and hatred. And other hearts yet to be mended. My next stop is to rescue a girl whose family died trying to protect her. She's alive only because the monster followed the scent of power to *this* world instead."

"Poor dear," Lizzie murmured.

"Lizzie speaks for us both," George added. "How can we help her?"

"On her world, the war is about to swallow the countryside. There'll be nowhere safe to leave her. Not there."

"You want us to take her in," Lizzie said quietly. "Would she even understand what was happening?"

"In all honesty," Dylan said, "I doubt she'll realize she's crossed worlds. She just needs—"

"A family," George finished for him.

Dylan nodded. "It won't be easy. I wouldn't ask if I didn't believe you two were her best chance at a future that isn't shaped by fear."

Lizzie breathed in, steady and resolved. "Our mother taught us that the more we have, the more responsible we are for others. It's why George brought Captain Meeks and Pathmaker here…even though I opposed it." She shook her head. "I was so wrong, Dylan. Fear made me selfish. Surviving this nightmare…well, it set my priorities straight. We don't have much. But we have this house. We have each other. And that is enough to share with someone in need."

"Here, here," George said, raising his mug. "May this home be a refuge to those who need one."

"When I come back with the girl," Dylan said, "I'll leave you to settle her in. Best I say my goodbyes now."

George rose and offered his hand.

"Our prayers go with you, Dylan Drake.

And if you ever need our help, you've only to ask."

"Thanks, George."

Lizzie hesitated, eyes down.

"I regret my mistrust deeply, Dylan. Ollie was right about you. I should have listened."

Dylan dipped his head until she met his gaze.

"We're good, Lizzie. Truly. I've enjoyed these months with you and George. Never had a sister of my own, but George is blessed to have you."

She kissed his cheek.

"Go with God, Dylan."

"Thank you. Mind if I use your cellar door?"

"Of course not," George said. "How long will you be?"

"Only a moment."

They watched him open the cellar door, vanish, then return almost instantly—this time with a teenaged girl at his side.

For a heartbeat, no one spoke. The fire

popped softly; Beaumont House seemed to hold its breath.

George and Lizzie stood frozen. The girl did not. She ran straight into their arms, clinging to them as if afraid they'd vanish if she let go. Lizzie wept openly.

Dylan hung back, letting the moment unfold.

"Dylan?" George finally asked, desperate for sense.

"Ask *her*," Dylan said gently.

George loosened his hold, cupped the girl's face, and stared.

"Ollie?"

Olivia Beaumont beamed at him, bright as dawn.

"Oh, George! When you and Lizzie hid me in the cellar, I was *so* frightened. I heard the crash upstairs and thought Beaumont House had fallen in."

"She stayed put, though," Dylan said. "Just like she promised. Door jammed a bit, that's all. I found her exactly where you'd left her."

"I thought I'd be trapped forever," Ollie said, shuddering. "Or that monster would come for me again."

"The monster is dead, Ollie," Dylan assured her. "Your brother, your sister, and I—along with a couple of good friends—we made sure of that."

"Lizzie," Ollie whispered, "why are you crying? I'm alright."

"We've just had a long night, dear," Lizzie managed. "Would you run upstairs and give us a moment? Dylan must leave, and we'd like to speak with him first."

"Of course." Ollie dipped a curtsey. "It was very nice to meet you, Dylan. Thank you for helping George and Lizzie."

"My pleasure," Dylan said. "Take good care of them."

Ollie hesitated a moment longer than necessary, studying his face as if trying to memorize it, then smiled and disappeared up the stairs.

Only once she was gone did Dylan speak plainly.

"Her George and Lizzie didn't survive the

night," Dylan explained. "Everything I told you about her was true. She's alone now. She just doesn't know it."

"And she thinks *we're* the George and Lizzie she knew?" George asked.

"That's right. Your worlds are the same story, told the same way," Dylan said. "Except for one quiet deviation."

Lizzie went very still.

"Her gift," Dylan said. "This Ollie never had it. She's just a sixteen-year-old girl hoping the war will end."

George said nothing, but Dylan thought he understood the question he was working over in his mind.

"She's not a substitute," Dylan assured them. "Your Ollie...was...one-of-a-kind. But she's gone. You'll still mourn her loss. How could you not?"

He rubbed at his chin and met Lizzie's gaze.

"But this Ollie needs you both...just like every Olivia Beaumont in every world needs her George and Lizzie."

"But we *aren't* her Lizzie and George," Lizzie added.

"That's true," Dylan said. "But it doesn't have to *stay* true. Right now, in this moment, you can choose to be hers. Call it providence or grace or just the Author's kindness, but you've been offered a second chance. Most of your memories will line up. And the rest?" He smiled faintly. "Time makes all memories a little fuzzy."

Lizzie touched her brother's arm. "George, she has no one."

George didn't answer right away. His jaw worked once, then stilled. He looked toward the stairs—toward the room where another Ollie now sat, turning pages with the same steady concentration he'd known since she was little. Two worlds, two sisters…and only one chance to keep that light alive.

"That isn't true," George said at last. "She has us. Ollie always has us."

Lizzie breathed out a shaky smile, relief softening her features.

They turned to thank their strange guest

but caught only a fleeting silhouette disappearing behind the cellar door. It was the last they ever saw of Dylan Drake. Yet Beaumont House remembered him—in its settled boards, its haunting silences, its rooms where his courage and kindness seemed to linger like a blessing.

Dylan Drake Adventures

"Monster/Hunter" in *Shadow Plays*
"The Witches of Greyfolk" in *The Witches of Greyfolk: Tales of the Evermore Book One*
(Coming Summer 2026)
"The Man Who Came to Help" in *Shadow Plays*
"The Christmas Cabin" in *The Christmas Cabin*
"The Eyes and Evan Richmond" in *All That Waits in the Night*
"Good Trouble" in *The Willing, The Wounded, and The Wizard*
"Interlude," "A Christmas Robbery" and "The Road to Christmas" in *The Christmas Cabin*
"Coffeehouse Confession" in *The Willing, The Wounded, and The Wizard*
Four Moments
"The Body in the Boat" in *A Wizard Restored: Tales of the Evermore Book Three*
(Coming Summer 2026)

Acknowledgments

The author would like to thank:

- The Author of *my* story, for daring to love even me.
- Heidi, my love and my friend.
- B., Ember, and Jacob, whose love and light make me so proud.
- The Theo Trio (Matt, Aaron, and Trey) and my Northside Christian Church family.
- The Imaginarium Convention, summer camp for my fellow authors.

J. Patrick Lemarr lives in Indiana with his wife, Heidi, and their children. When he isn't crafting horror and fantasy, he is writing exclusive content for his Patreon supporters. Learn more at www.jpatricklemarr.com.

patreon.com/jpatricklemarr

amazon.com/author/jpatricklemarr

goodreads.com/jpatricklemarr

facebook.com/theofficialjpatricklemarr

x.com/jpatricklemarr

instagram.com/jpatricklemarr

threads.com/@jpatricklemarr

Also by J Patrick Lemarr

The Witches of Greyfolk: Tales of the Evermore Book One
A Secret Sin, A Silent Sea: Tales of the Evermore Book Two
Shadow Plays
All That Waits in the Night
The Christmas Cabin
The Willing, The Wounded, and The Wizard
The Figure
Four Moments: A Dylan Drake Story
A Wizard Restored: Tales of the Evermore Book Three